It's a Duke's life

Sequel to 'Don't flatter yourself'

A P&P spin-off

Sydney Salier

This is a work of fiction. The characters, locations, and events portrayed in this book are fictitious or are used fictitiously. Any similarity to real persons, living or dead is purely coincidental and not intended by the author.

To Michael

As always, thanks

Sydney Salier

CONTENTS

List of major characters vi

1   Cambridge 1

2   Higher Learning 7

3   New friends 14

4   Which brother? 19

5   Lieutenant Flinter 26

6   Reciprocity 28

7   Love Hurts 35

8   London Season 45

9   Duke of Denton 49

10 Return to Denton House 53

11 Games 59

12 Overtures 66

13 Apologies 72

14 Wedding 78

15 Again? 83

16 Getting acquainted 90

17 Prodigal 95

18 Proposal 102

19 Family Council 107

20 Big Guns 113

21 Plans 119

22 Education 125

23 Surprise 134

24 Introductions 138

25 Preparations 145

26 Denton Ball 149

27 Happy Ending? 154

Books by Sydney Salier 156

List of major characters

Alistair Flinter	Marquess of Denmere
	Later the Duke of Denton
Lord Robert Flinter	Twin brother of Alistair
Amelia Flinter	Dowager Duchess of Denton
	Grandmother of the Duke of Denton
Charlotte Lucas	Friend of Lady Elizabeth Darcy
Fitzwilliam Darcy	Master of Pemberley, Derbyshire
	Husband of Lady Elizabeth
Lady Elizabeth Darcy	Daughter of Earl Fellmar and Lady Francine
	Wife of Fitzwilliam Darcy
Thomas Bennet	Master of Longbourn, Meryton, Hertfordshire
	Second husband of Lady Francine Flinter
Mrs (Lady) Francine Bennet	nee Flinter, second wife of Thomas Bennet,
	Daughter of the Duke and Duchess of Denton
	First husband was Earl Fellmar
Lady Alexandra Hunt	Friend of Alistair
Lady Beatrice	The Countess of Marven
	Aunt and Guardian for Lady Alexandra
Richard Fitzwilliam	Cousin to Mr Darcy
Jane Fitzwilliam	Daughter of Thomas Bennet and his first wife
	Wife of Richard Fitzwilliam
Lady Susan Fitzwilliam	Mother of Colonel Richard Fitzwilliam, aunt of Mr Darcy
Andrew Fitzwilliam, Earl of Matlock	Father of Colonel Richard Fitzwilliam, uncle of Mr Darcy
Lady Catherine de Bourgh	Sister of the Earl of Matlock, Aunt of Mr Darcy & Richard Fitzwilliam, patroness of Mr Collins
Anne de Bourgh	Daughter of Lady Catherine
	Cousin of Mr Darcy and Richard Fitzwilliam
William Collins	Cousin to Mr Bennet, former heir presumptive to Longbourn
Sir William Lucas	Father of Charlotte Lucas, a community leader in Meryton
Mary Bennet	Daughter of Thomas Bennet and Lady Francine
Catherine Bennet (Kitty)	Daughter of Thomas Bennet and Lady Francine
Lydia Bennet	Daughter of Thomas Bennet and Lady Francine

1 Cambridge

1800

Alistair, Marquess of Denmere and his twin brother Lord Robert Flinter arrived in Cambridge for the Michaelmas term in style.

Their grandmother, the Dowager Duchess of Denton, had decided to see them settled into university like she had done for them at Eton. Therefore, they arrived in the Denton's best carriage, while their main luggage followed separately.

The Dowager had arranged private lodgings for the boys, as she thought of them. At the age of seventeen years, they, of course, preferred the term young men.

The Earl of Matlock, whose nineteen-year-old second son Richard currently attended Cambridge, had recommended the boarding house.

When they disembarked from the carriage, they were greeted by a pleasant-looking middle-aged woman who was dressed plainly but well. 'Welcome to Huntington House. I am Mrs Huntington.' She smiled at all the newcomers. 'You must be Her Grace, the Dowager Duchess of Denton.' At the Duchess' nod, she continued, 'please come in. I have the rooms prepared. I will show you to them directly. They are very pleasant rooms; I am certain you will like them.' Without giving anyone a chance to say anything, she bustled into the house and up the stairs, leaving the others to follow.

The Dowager and her grandsons exchanged amused looks. 'I believe we had better follow your landlady.' The lady suggested with a barely suppressed grin.

When they caught up with Mrs Huntington, she was opening the door to a very pleasant sitting room, which had doors leading off to each side. 'As you requested, this suite has two bedrooms. There is also a dressing room where your valet can sleep. Or he can share the servants' quarters.'

The Dowager interjected, 'Parker is used to having a room to himself.'

Mrs Huntington looked surprised. 'You must be treating your servants exceptionally well. Let me think. I do have a small room available at the end of the corridor here, but it was intended for a young gentleman...'

'Is that room promised to anyone?' asked the Dowager.

'No, it is not at the moment. It is just that I have to charge you for it separately. My patrons usually do not wish to go to that expense for their servants...' Mrs Huntington said uncertainly.

'It is settled then; Parker will have that room.' The Dowager was satisfied. Good servants deserved to be treated well. Although the Dowager was rather enlightened in her treatment of her servants, she was not wholly altruistic. Contented servants also gave better service and loyalty to a considerate employer.

In the meantime, Alistair and Robert explored the rooms and settled on who was to get which bedroom.

They had just returned to the sitting room when another resident of Huntington House came up the stairs. He stopped at the open door. When he saw the brothers, he announced, 'ah, the Denton Doubles have arrived. Richard Fitzwilliam at your service.' He made an elaborate bow.

Alistair found his attitude engaging and bowed just as elaborately. 'You are entirely correct, Mr Fitzwilliam. I am Alistair Flinter, and this is my brother Robert,' Alistair replied. 'But we are neglecting the proper courtesies.' Turning to the Dowager Duchess, he bowed again. 'Grandmother, I would like you to meet Richard Fitzwilliam. Mr Fitzwilliam, this is our grandmother, the Dowager Duchess of Denton.'

Fitzwilliam bowed to the Dowager. 'Your Grace, please forgive my discourtesy. I am most honoured to make your acquaintance,' he finished with a charming smile.

The Dowager smiled, 'for the sake of your father, you are forgiven. If only you could keep these rapscallions out of trouble, I would be forever in your debt.'

'My father has tasked me with the same assignment, although he thought *they* might be a good influence on *me*,' Richard replied with twinkling eyes.

'I see you are all birds of a feather. Very well, I will have to rely on the modicum of good sense that was drummed into all of you, to keep you out of too much trouble.' The Dowager sensed that despite his light-hearted words, Richard Fitzwilliam was a reliable young man. 'I shall leave you to get acquainted. I will see you before I return to London in a few days.'

~~DL~~

After the Dowager had left, Robert addressed Fitzwilliam. 'It is good to see you again, Richard.'

'You two know each other?' asked Alistair in surprise.

'We met at Eton,' supplied Richard. 'Since we are both younger sons we were mostly ignored by the, ah...

'Snotty first-born louts you favoured until Lizzy took you down a peg,' Robert told Alistair.

'That sounds like an interesting story,' said Richard, dropping into a chair, 'tell me more. Who is Lizzy and how did she manage to humanise one of the Lords?' Richard asked, using the nickname the younger sons had given the coterie of heirs who were putting on airs and making life miserable for the younger boys.

'Lizzy is our young cousin Elizabeth. When we first met her, which must have been just around the time you left Eton, she was six years old. Alistair mistook her for a servant's daughter and acted accordingly. She gave him a tongue-lashing that was a joy to behold,' Robert explained with a smirk before his brother could object.

'Bested by a six-year-old? I would have loved to have been a witness,' laughed Richard. 'I had heard that you suddenly became human and wondered what had happened.'

'Now, would you like me to show you around today or would you like to wait until tomorrow?' Richard asked, becoming all brisk mentor.

'Having been stuck in a carriage all day, I would like a chance to stretch my legs. But only after I get cleaned up,' responded Alistair.

'Give us an hour to become fit for human company. Then we can go out and give Parker a chance to get everything organised. That way we can avoid his complaints about us getting underfoot,' suggested Robert.

'An hour it is,' agreed Richard, who left the room with a wave.

'Did you have to tell him about Lizzy?' complained Alistair.

'Considering how rude you were to him at Eton, yes, I did.'

'I can only hope that Richard knows how to keep his mouth shut. Unlike some brother, who shall remain nameless.'

~~DL~~

As agreed, Richard returned an hour later. 'Are you ready to go exploring?' he asked. Since the brothers were indeed ready, they set off for a walk around town.

In between pointing out the various sights, Richard also doled out snippets of information and advice.

'Mrs Huntington sets a fine table, but if you want to eat out, I suggest you try the Cock and Magpie. The food is good, the wine is not watered unless you want it to be, and the patrons are generally well behaved.'

He showed them the various colleges where they could take lessons. 'You will hear some of the other students tell you that there is no need to study because as long as your school fees are paid, you will receive your degree. I suggest you do not listen to them. While it is true up to a point, they are also part of the fast crowd. That group consists mostly of the first sons. The "Lords" from Eton. All they are interested in is drinking, gambling, and whoring.'

Richard shook his head, thinking about the titled louts he had encountered. 'If you hang around with them, all you end up with is a sore head, empty pockets and the French disease. None of which are pleasant.'

The brothers thought of their father's example and were inclined to agree with Richard.

While pointing out various other landmarks, Richard informed them that 'about half the students here are for the church. You had better watch out for the tuft-hunters. According to my brother, they can be quite a nuisance. We have only one advowson, but the vicar is getting

4

old, so every other younger son wants to be friends in the hope to receive the living.'

'Should we worry about you trying to get our favour for one of our advowsons?' Alistair asked with a grin.

'You are safe from me. I am for the army as soon as I reach my majority.' Richard laughed. 'I prefer the excitement of serving my country to serving god. I am also not enough of a hypocrite to preach sermons that I do not necessarily believe in.'

'Are you an atheist?' Alistair asked, concerned.

'No, I simply disagree with some of the interpretations the less educated students try to foist off onto their parishioners. Personally, I think they are simply trying to present their own opinions as the word of god. And some of those opinions...' he shrugged his shoulders.

'Do you like chess?' Richard wanted to know. When both brothers agreed, he told them, 'in that case I will take you to our chess club. You will find good company there.'

They strolled on taking in the sights.

'You just missed the excitement,' Richard told the brothers. 'Cambridge is still abuzz with the news that it is getting a new college. Sir George Downing left his fortune to establish a college and King George just granted the Royal Charter for the Downing College.'

'Why do they need another college? From what you said, students mostly do not learn anything in the colleges they already have,' Robert asked.

'It is getting a little better. In Cambridge, you can now get an honours degree for which you actually have to pass a rather stringent examination. I suppose one of these days students will come here mostly to study.' Richard grinned. 'In the meantime, why not enjoy both learning and socialising.'

Richard stopped in front of a building. 'Here we are. This is where our chess club meets.' He led them inside.

'This is a pub,' Robert noted.

'Very observant of you. Here you can combine playing chess and having a drink. The drinks are a bit dearer, but they are good. The landlord prefers you leaving moderately sober. It saves on furniture. Which is why he welcomes chess players.'

'Good. I hate pointless fights.'

'Good evening, Mr Fitzwilliam. I see you have brought some new friends. Will they be joining you upstairs?' the landlord greeted the trio.

'Yes, Mr Porthouse, I found another couple of chess players. Mr Flinter and Mr Flinter.' Richard introduced them by their preferred names.

'Welcome gentlemen. I hope you enjoy our hospitality.' He bustled off.

'Shall we?' Richard indicated the stairs. 'Battle awaits.'

~~DL~~

2   Higher Learning

1801

As the weeks flew by, the brothers settled into their new life.

They attended lectures, learned about strategy at the chess club and mostly stayed out of trouble.

They made some new friends, reconnected with a few old friends from Eton and as much as possible ignored the people they did not like.

One evening while the brothers and Richard were having a nightcap in their rooms after an evening spent at the chess club, Robert appeared rather thoughtful.

'What is on your mind, little brother,' Alistair teased. 'You look like you are trying to solve the problems of the world.'

'I am not trying to solve any problems. I was simply thinking about the people with whom we just spent the evening.' Robert suddenly grinned. 'Are you aware that you are the odd one out, *big brother*?'

'What do you mean?' Alistair was puzzled. 'I play chess as well or as badly as most of them. I do not believe I act any different than any of them. I probably drank a little more tonight than I should have, just like they did. That was probably the reason why I exceeded my normal limit. I expect I will regret that in the morning like they will. Except, of course, Browning, who can drink like a fish and never suffers for it.'

'All this is true, which makes you even odder. What think you, Richard?' Robert teased.

'I thought Alistair was odd, ever since you arrived at Cambridge. I do not think he has changed much since then,' Richard replied.

'This makes it even better,' laughed Robert. 'Neither of you has realised that amongst our friends Alistair is the only heir. The rest of us are all spares. Yet he does not look down his nose at us.'

'That is what has been odd about him,' cried Richard. 'He has acted like a human being rather than one of the Lords.'

'My point precisely. Am I the only man in our circles who is blessed with a decent older brother?'

'Mine is not too bad. A little stuffy perhaps, but otherwise quite decent.'

'Maybe so but look at the crop of heirs gracing the colleges. On those odd occasions when they grace the college, that is. Can you think of a single first-born here, who is not a wastrel?

'My cousin Darcy is as honourable as they come,' supplied Richard.

'But he is not here. The rest of them are full of their own... self-importance,' argued Robert.

'They are full of something else too,' supplied Alistair. 'Which is why I prefer your company to theirs.'

'You have the right of it there,' laughed Richard.

They all toasted their agreement... repeatedly.

~~DL~~

A few months later, Alistair's attitude won him the respect of some unexpected people.

He and his brother were having dinner with Richard at the Cock and Magpie, where the food was as good as Richard had promised. They were having a pleasant meal and were chatting comfortably when there was a commotion.

Gerald Stone, Viscount Braxton and a group of his cronies, were making a nuisance of themselves. Braxton was loudly complaining that the serving girl had spilled his drink. He neglected to mention that she spilled the drink when he had slapped her on the behind.

Alistair could not tolerate the abuse Braxton was heaping on the frightened girl. He stood up and confronted the bully. 'Stop abusing the girl. It was your doing that she spilled the drink.'

'What is it to you? Are you interested in the little slut?' Braxton sneered.

'I am interested in the fact that you are giving our class a bad name by behaving like a drunken bully.' Alistair was fighting to rein in his temper.

'Who cares what they think. They are beneath men such as you or I,' Braxton declared.

Richard whispered to the landlord, 'send a boy to find a proctor.'

The man looked relieved and hurried to follow the suggestion.

Meanwhile, Alistair was in full swing. 'What makes you think you are better than these hard-working, decent and law-abiding people.'

Braxton blustered, 'I am a gentleman. I do not have to sully my hands with work.'

Alistair looked him up and down and drawled, 'there are a couple of points I would like you to consider. The expression gentleman implies a man with exquisite manners, who is polite and gracious to all. Not a drunken lout who abuses his position.'

'So says the man whose own father spends his time drinking and whoring,' sneered Braxton.

'Maybe so. But even on his worst day his manners are ten times better than yours. And he never abuses his position.'

Alistair shrugged casually. 'Be that as it may, my father is not here making a spectacle of himself. You are. And you interrupted the second point I was trying to make.' Alistair had overheard that help had been sent for, so he continued to play for time.

'If it were not for people like these, working your father's estate and paying their rents, you would not have money to throw around. And allowing you to think you can call yourself a gentleman. Instead of treating these people with disdain, you should be grateful that someone is prepared to clean up after you. If it were not for people like these, working as servants, you would have to do your own cooking, cleaning and whatever else they do for you.'

Now Alistair smiled grimly. 'There is something else you should learn. Respect can only be earned, not commanded. If you treat people with respect, they, in turn, will respect you. If you do not, they will not. And all the bullying and blustering in the world will not change that.'

'Well said, my Lord. Maybe these so-called gentlemen will consider your advice while they cool their heels in the Dean's office.' Proctor Hill stepped up to stand next to Alistair.

'Gentlemen,' he sarcastically addressed Braxton and his cronies, 'you are in violation of the rules of the College. No cap, no gowns, out past gating hours and making a nuisance of yourselves. Not behaving like proper gentlemen at all. I think you will have plenty of opportunity to consider the error of your ways. You will now come with me and leave these good people to enjoy their evening. Yours is over.'

He turned, offered a, 'good night, my Lord,' to Alistair and walked out of the room with a polite nod at the landlord and the other guests.

Braxton looked like he wanted to argue, but one of his friends was sober enough to whisper, 'do not make it worse than it is.' This comment brought him to his senses and, drawing himself up to his full height and giving Alistair a disdainful look, he followed the proctor.

As soon as they had left the room, the landlord hurried over. 'Thank you for your assistance, my Lord. You are a true *gentleman*.' The man smiled when he emphasised the word. 'Would you do me the honour of accepting this wine as my thanks?' He presented a bottle to Alistair.

'Your thanks and the wine are not necessary. But we will use it to drink to your health,' Alistair declared.

The landlord poured the wine for the trio, who toasted him and congratulated him on the excellence of the food and wine.

The landlord had left when Alistair and his friends were interrupted again. This time by an older gentleman at the next table. 'My congratulations on your handling of the situation, gentlemen. Allow me to introduce myself. I am General Bryant.'

'A pleasure to meet you, General. I am Alistair Flinter, Marquess of Denmere, and these gentlemen are my brother Robert and our friend Richard Fitzwilliam. But I wonder... my brother and I were fortunate to have a Mr David Bryant, originally of Impington, as our mentor while growing up. Are you perchance related to him?'

The General smiled. 'It is indeed a small world. He is a distant cousin of mine, although our families have not been close for many years.'

The name had also caught Richard's attention. 'Are you the General Bryant who...'

'Yes, yes. That was me. But it was a long time ago.' The General smiled amicably. 'I gather you are a student of military history, Mr Fitzwilliam?'

'Yes, Sir, I am. I am hoping to get a commission in the army when I reach my majority,' Richard agreed.

'I liked the way you called for reinforcements. That was quick and sensible thinking. The army can use men like you. When you are ready, drop me a note, and I will put you in touch with the right people,' the General smiled.

He then turned to Alistair. 'Lord Denmere, please do not think me patronising when I say that I appreciate you standing up for the girl. It is refreshing that someone from the nobility sees the value in ordinary people. Some of the best men under my command have come from humble beginnings, and they excelled when given a chance to show what they are capable of. Please never forget this.' He smiled at the young men. 'Now I have interrupted your dinner long enough. I wish you a good night, and please give my regards to your mentor when next you speak to him.'

The trio turned back to their dinner.

'That was interesting,' Robert commented. '

Richard grinned. 'It seems there is yet hope for the nobility. Cheers.'

~~DL~~

'Why are you looking so despondent?' Alistair asked his brother, who was staring blankly into the fire of their sitting room, where he was lounging in a chair. They had recently returned from a pleasant dinner with Richard, hosted by the Earl of Matlock.

'Seeing Richard with his father, reminded me again that we do not truly have a father. Ours has been conspicuous by his absence all our lives.'

'We may not have had a father, but we had people who cared about us. You know that most of the children in our class are raised by nurses, governesses, and tutors. Compared to them, we were blessed.'

~~DL~~

He and Alistair had had an idyllic childhood. Being twins, they always had a companion with whom to get into mischief.

It was also populated by several loving people. Foremost was their grandmother. In the earliest years, they also had the company of their aunt, who was very good at enacting historical battles with toy soldiers. But when the boys were seven years of age, their aunt went away and only infrequently visited. They learned that she now had a family of her own and needed to spend time with them.

There was also the time when David Bryant had been a frequent visitor. He always had time for the boys. To play with them and answer their myriad of questions. Robert realised that Bryant had been the closest father figure they had known.

He even visited after they had gone to Eton. Bryant always made a point of spending time with the brothers. Much of the best advice had come from that man.

Robert remembered the discussion they had had when he discovered that girls were delightfully different.

'Treat them with respect,' Bryant had advised. 'Better yet truly respect them. Society does not give them many options, other than look pretty and catch a husband as soon as possible. But if you respect them and their opinions, they might allow you to see beneath the surface, and you may find astonishing minds and personalities. That is the best part.' He had smiled sarcastically. 'Of course, just as with men, some are stupid as stumps. But if you still treat them with respect, you should be able to find that out before you make any binding decisions.'

That advice had stuck. It made social situations much more enjoyable. It gave him topics of conversation which were enjoyable to both parties. Rather than commenting on the weather or gossiping about mutual acquaintances.

It was also fun to see the reaction of the ladies when he asked their opinions about books they might have read. Or even if they were interested in current affairs. As in politics, not mistresses and lovers of their acquaintances.

All this was thanks to David Bryant. His own father might not have taken an interest in his sons, but there was at least one man who had taken a fatherly interest and given the best advice he could.

Robert determined that he had been remiss in his correspondence with Bryant, but he would rectify that immediately.

~~DL~~

3   New friends

1802

Alistair and Robert were getting ready for yet another assembly. This one was being hosted by the university. Their valet, Parker, was ensuring that both young gentlemen were impeccably turned out in identical ensembles.

'You know, I truly miss Richard,' Alistair commented to his brother.

'Yes, I know. He was fun to have around the last two years. But as he said, we are big boys now, and we do not need him as a nursemaid any longer.' Robert grinned.

'The impudence of the man,' asserted Alistair in mock offence, 'to suggest we could not have taken care of ourselves. After all, there are two of us and only one of him.'

'I am only glad that his cousin and his cousin's shadow were not around. Just think of the fun we would have missed out on if Richard had to have looked after Darcy. That young man is such a stuffed shirt. But I hope he realises soon what his shadow is getting up to. They have only been here for two months, and Wickham is already getting a reputation as a wastrel.'

'Ah...' Parker attracted the brother's attention.

'What do you know that we do not, Parker?' Robert asked.

'According to what I have heard, Mr Darcy might already be wise to the character of Mr Wickham,' Parker informed them. 'Mr Wickham is switching accommodation with a Mr Charles Bingley. Apparently, Mr Wickham objects to Mr Darcy's repressive ways. And Mr Darcy prefers propriety.'

'That does not surprise me in the least. I cannot imagine two more different characters,' commented Alistair. 'Darcy might be rather straitlaced, but he appears honourable. Wickham, on the other hand, is rather too fond of the fast crowd.'

'Well, neither of them is our problem. The lovely ladies at tonight's assembly are much more interesting,' replied Robert.

~~DL~~

Alistair was having a wonderful time. By pretending to be Robert, he had a chance to converse with the young ladies, without having to endure the fawning that ladies usually inflicted on an heir. The spare was spared the attention of matchmaking mothers and could enjoy himself.

Although he was afraid that their ruse would not last forever, he would take advantage of the reprieve. Admittedly, his current dance partner was delightful and seemed unimpressed by wealth and titles since she herself had both and was not in need of either.

'Lady Alexandra, pray tell how you come to the exceptional attitude of not caring for rank?'

'My father taught me to be more interested in a person's character than their station. I find that to be excellent advice. It should help me to avoid fortune hunters when I officially come out in the next London season.' Alexandra explained.

'Your father must be an exceptional man. I admit, I quite agree with you. According to my brother, fortune hunters of either sex are the bane of our existence.' Alistair sighed theatrically. 'I would much rather be a poor but happy second son, than a miserable heir trapped into a marriage I did not choose.'

'It must be very difficult for your brother then,' Alexandra replied sympathetically.

'Indeed, it is. It is difficult enough for myself since some people mistake me for my brother. Whenever they do, I am subjected to the same fawning that he has to endure.

'You poor man,' laughed Alexandra, 'to have to endure the attentions of many beautiful and accomplished young ladies.'

'Please do not laugh, my Lady. You just wait until *you* have to listen to descriptions of the weather for six hours straight,' protested Alistair.

'Touché,' acknowledged Lady Alexandra.

~~DL~~

Alistair and Robert were coming back into the ballroom from having been outside for a breath of fresh air, when they came across Lady Alexandra being importuned by none other than George Wickham and his new crony, Gerald Stone, Viscount Braxton.

'I am sorry, sir, I cannot dance with you since we have not been formally introduced.' Lady Alexandra said as she tried to sidestep Wickham to return to her aunt's side.

Wickham blocked her and in his most ingratiating manner said, 'My Lady, one does not need a formal introduction in a ballroom simply to dance. Please do me the honour of the next dance.'

'Wickham, you heard the lady. She does not wish to dance with someone she does not know.' Alistair stepped up to Alexandra's side and faced Wickham.

'You know the lady?' asked Braxton.

'I have had the honour of an *introduction*,' replied Alistair coldly.

'Splendid,' exclaimed Braxton. 'Since you know us as well, you can introduce us.'

'My Lady, do you wish to be introduced to these persons?' asked Alistair in his most polite manner.

'I would be most happy to be introduced to *gentlemen*,' Alexandra replied with her sweetest smile. 'Since there are none present, to whom I have not already been introduced, I would rather return to my aunt. If you would be so kind as to escort me?' she asked Alistair.

Braxton exclaimed, 'you little...' and tried to grab Alexandra's arm, only to find his wrist held by Robert, who had been standing unnoticed behind him.

'My dear boy, it is not gentlemanlike to try to grab a lady,' Robert purred.

"My Lady,' Alistair said while offering Alexandra his arm with a small bow.

'Thank you, Sir,' she answered politely, taking the proffered arm.

Alistair, with a challenging look at Wickham, led the lady away.

Braxton shook off Robert's restraining hand. 'You are welcome to her, she is too scrawny for my taste anyway,' and walked away trying to regain his composure, while Wickham tried to appear nonchalant as he followed Braxton.

Robert watched them for a moment to ensure they headed in the opposite direction, then followed after his brother. He caught up with Alistair and Alexandra, just as they reached the Countess of Marven.

'Thank you for rescuing my niece, Lord Robert.' Lady Beatrice addressed Alistair. 'Judging by your looks, you must be Lord Denmere,' she smiled at Robert. 'Thank you also for your assistance.'

Alistair quickly glanced around and judged that they had privacy. 'Lady Beatrice, I must apologise for a small deception. Would you allow me to introduce my brother, Lord Robert Flinter?'

Lady Beatrice smiled graciously. 'I am delighted to meet you, Sir. Alexandra, I would like you to meet Lord Robert Flinter,' the countess indicated Robert with twinkling eyes, 'and I believe you already know Alistair, Marquess of Denmere.'

Alexandra curtsied somewhat impertinently and acknowledged the introduction, 'it is my pleasure to meet you, Sirs.'

The countess smiled mischievously. 'I must congratulate you on your fortune to have an identical brother. Considering how practised you are, I would guess this is not the first time you both act as each other?'

'Alistair hates being hunted, so I let him use my name when he needs to.' Robert grinned at the ladies, who appeared amused rather than offended that they had been fooled.

Alexandra laughed at Alistair. 'No wonder you are so familiar with the trials of being prey. But I must add my thanks for your timely rescue. Who were those men?'

'They were Gerald Stone, Viscount Braxton and George Wickham, sycophant of Braxton. Wickham's father is the steward at Pemberley. I presume you know of the Darcy estate in Derbyshire?' Alistair explained.

'I am familiar with the names of Darcy and Braxton,' Lady Beatrice replied. 'To the best of my knowledge, they are the opposites of each other. Mr Wickham I had obviously not heard of, but considering the company he keeps...'

'According to my information, you are correct, my lady,' Alistair confirmed her unvoiced suspicions. 'Although, I admit I was surprised at how persistent Wickham was. He has a reputation to prefer easy prey.'

'He may have been trying to show off to Braxton,' surmised Robert.

'In that case, I am doubly grateful for your assistance,' Alexandra said. 'To both of you.'

'Any time,' the brothers said in unison. 'It was our pleasure. We enjoy foiling scoundrels and rescuing damsels in distress,' Robert continued.

Alexandra smiled at the brothers. 'Let us make a pact then. Whenever we are in company, we will rescue each other from tedious conversation, fortune-hunters and scoundrels.'

'A pact it is,' agreed Alistair with a grin.

~~DL~~

4   Which brother?

1802

A few weeks later saw the whole family, except for the Duke, gathered at Denton Manor for Christmas.

The Dowager was in her element, organising everyone to ensure that they had as much fun as possible. She loved the laughter of children in the house.

Unlike most of her peers, who were too busy with presenting a polished front to society to have any interest in their children, she was confident of her position and could afford to indulge herself with their company. The children, of course, not her peers who often bored her.

Mrs Bennet constantly had to put her foot down to stop her mother from being too extravagant with her gifts to the children.

Alistair and Robert, who were not above eavesdropping when it suited them, thought it was hilarious listening to the battle of wills being fought between their grandmother and their aunt.

Alistair was impressed, 'Aunt Francine must be the only person in the country willing and able to stand up to grandmother. I must admit, when she is determined to have her way, grandmother even frightens me a little.'

Robert laughed, 'I am very happy to hear you say that because I feel the same way. But no matter how valiantly Aunt Francine stands her ground, grandmother will win in the end.'

Alistair disagreed, 'you heard grandmother. She agreed not to give the girls ponies.'

Robert corrected him, 'I heard her agree not to give the girls ponies *this year*.'

Alistair looked startled and then started laughing. 'Oh dear. I wonder if Aunt Francine realised.'

'She probably did. But I think she knows that she will not win in the long run but argues because she knows how much grandmother loves it when someone stands up to her. Politely and intelligently, of course.'

'Is that why you argue with her so much?' Alistair was stunned.

'Of course. I thought you knew. But I also have enough sense not to argue about anything important. Because then she can become rather intimidating. But apart from that, it is a game,' Robert grinned.

'Does grandmother know you are deliberately baiting her?'

'I expect she does. Do not forget, she is an intelligent woman. We are simply both sharpening our skills at debate.'

Alistair was rather thoughtful for a minute. 'Why do I get the impression that you are more intelligent than I am?'

'Probably because I am,' was the impertinent reply.

~~DL~~

At dinner that night, they kept the family amused with tall tales from their time at university.

While he was as amused as the others, Mr Bennet could not help but caution the twins. 'I understand that you enjoy being the conquering heroes, but keep in mind that you are not ten feet tall and bulletproof. I would like you to exercise at least a modicum of forethought.'

'Do not worry overmuch, Uncle. Grandmother has been diligent in teaching us to pick our battles,' replied Robert. 'I also learnt even more about strategy from Aunt Francine and Mr Bryant.'

'You learnt strategy from my wife?' Mr Bennet was shocked.

'When we re-enacted battles with toy soldiers, she often related the strategies of battles to the strategies employed by the *ton*. It made for an interesting education,' explained Alistair.

'I had never thought to apply battle strategies to the manoeuvrings of the *ton*,' admitted Bennet.

'You were not raised to deal with them. When I learned about history, it was simply obvious to me, and I decided I did not wish to live in a war zone,' shrugged Mrs Bennet.

Even the Dowager was a little startled to hear her daughter liken the jockeying for position with a war zone. 'You never mentioned this opinion before. I must admit, you are not far off the mark. But speaking of Mr Bryant reminds me that Mr Cartwright has extended an invitation to you to a ball he is giving next week,' the Dowager addressed the brothers. 'Mr Bryant will be there as well.'

'I would love to see Mr Bryant again. It has been ages since his last visit,' Robert enthused.

'It is settled then. I will send your acceptance.'

~~DL~~

'There is no need to be so reticent, Lord Denmere. Lady Fitzmichael pointed you out to me earlier. You do not have to pretend with me,' Miss Dullar cooed at Robert.

'I am sorry to disappoint you, but Lady Fitzmichael mistook me for my brother. I am Robert Flinter,' Robert tried to explain yet again.

'Of course, *Mister Flinter*. I quite understand.' Miss Dullar was obviously not convinced, but since she was a pretty dancer, Robert resolved to enjoy the dance.

'Is this not a splendid ball, Mister Flinter. I do so enjoy dancing in such wonderful surroundings. I find that private balls are so much better than those crowds one encounters at public balls.'

'You are quite correct, Miss Dullar, I have rarely attended such an excellent assembly.' Robert was happy that at least she did not speak about the weather.

'Everyone here is exceedingly fashionable, unlike the assemblies I attended in Bristol.' Miss Dullar prattled on. 'Although I must admit, I prefer the weather at Bristol. I think the breeze off the ocean is so wonderfully invigorating.'

Robert barely suppressed a groan when she mentioned the weather. 'Since I have never been to Bristol, I will accept that you are the expert on this subject, Miss Dullar. But I have been meaning to ask, do you enjoy reading books?'

'Dear me, no. Do you think me a bluestocking? I can assure you I am no such thing. I much rather occupy my time with embroidery. It is so soothing to stitch while having a conversation with friends.'

'Do you not even read novels, Miss Dullar? I understand that many ladies enjoy to divert themselves with such a pastime,' Robert tried again.

'I assure you, Lord Denmere, I have no such interests,' protested Miss Dullar.

Robert was spared a retort, to yet again explain her confusion about his name, when the music stopped. Instead, he offered to fetch some punch for the lady to escape her vapid conversation, at least for a short time.

'That is exceedingly kind of you, Sir, but I feel rather too warm at present. A breath of fresh air on the balcony would be just the thing.' She latched on to his arm.

Robert did not have a choice but to escort her to the balcony. At the door he managed to disengage her hand from his arm to maximise the distance between them. To no avail. As soon as she stepped through the door, she turned around and threw herself at him.

'Oh, you are so wicked, Lord Denmere. To take advantage of an innocent maiden like myself.' Miss Dullar cooed, apparently unaware that Robert had immediately put his hands behind his back, which could be seen from the ballroom.

'Miss Dullar, as you are perfectly well aware, I did not touch you except to pry your hand off my arm.'

'But I could tell that you wanted to ravish me.'

'Contrary to what you claimed, I believe you have read too many vulgar novels.' Robert held on to his temper and determinedly kept his arms clasped behind his back. 'I can assure you no gentleman would consider ravishing you.' *Since two minutes of your prattle would put him to sleep,* he thought.

She stepped away from him. 'No matter. Since I am now compromised, you will have to do the gentlemanly thing and marry me, Lord Denmere. I will go and speak to my father immediately. He will ensure that you do your duty.' Miss Dullar stormed off in search of her parent.

'I see you managed to attract another fortune hunter,' a laughing voice said behind Robert.

'Mr Bryant, it is good to see you again, especially under the circumstances. Would it be too much to hope that you witnessed the entire situation?' Robert greeted the gentleman.

'You are in luck again,' smiled David Bryant. 'By the bye, which one are you?'

'Robert Flinter at your service,' said Robert and gave an elaborate bow.

'We had better go and find Mr Dullar. Better nip this in the bud. He will not be best pleased that his daughter made a fool of herself, throwing herself at a penniless and untitled gentleman. But the young lady is not known for her intelligence.' David Bryant put a hand on Robert's shoulder and guided him in the wake of Miss Dullar.

They met up with father and daughter near the door to the cardroom.

'There is my intended,' cried Miss Dullar.

'I am glad that you have come to your senses young man and came to me. I would hate to have to go looking for you,' said a big, blustery man of middle years.

'Mr Dullar, I presume?' asked David Bryant.

'I am he.'

'I am Mr Bryant. I believe there has been some misunderstanding. Just because a young lady trips and holds on to a gentleman to find her balance, does not mean she is compromised.'

'But she is compromised when he grabs her and tries to ravish her. I will see Lord Denmere do his duty and make things right for my daughter,' Dullar insisted.

'Mr Dullar, I witnessed the whole scene. It is impossible for a man to ravish a woman when his hands are clasped behind his back.'

'That is an unlikely story. My daughter says he compromised her; therefore, he will marry her,' Dullar blustered.

'You are correct; it is an unlikely story.' David Bryant admitted, and Dullar started to look satisfied. 'I was hoping to spare your daughter her blushes by claiming she tripped. But I now see that only the truth will do.'

David Bryant sighed dramatically. 'I am very much afraid that your daughter did not trip at all but threw herself at Lord Robert.'

'Who the devil is Lord Robert?' asked Dullar.

'I am,' replied Robert.

'No, you are the Marquess of Denmere,' both Mr and Miss Dullar insisted.

'As a matter of fact, he is Lord Robert, and I am the Marquess of Denmere,' came a drawling voice from behind Dullar.

Mr Dullar and his daughter turned around and looked on in astonishment as Alistair stepped out of the cardroom. 'What is going on here? Why is my name being bandied about?'

Dullar found his voice sooner than his daughter did. 'There are two of you?'

'I know it is confusing. People often claim they cannot tell us apart. But it should be obvious, I am much more handsome than my brother,' Alistair claimed.

'Now that we have established the identity of the person Miss Dullar threw herself at,' David Bryant returned to the business at hand while Dullar bristled, 'do you still insist on my telling the truth about this incident. Or would you prefer the polite fiction?'

'If you tell people that my daughter threw herself at Lord Robert, she would be ruined.' Dullar was aghast.

'But it is the truth as you insisted.'

Dullar turned to his daughter. 'Why did you throw yourself at the gentleman?'

'I wanted to be a duchess,' wailed Miss Dullar.

'Gentlemen, I believe the *accident* has made my daughter overwrought. I need to take her home.' All the fight had gone out of Mr Dullar. 'Thank you for your assistance. Goodbye.'

After he left David Bryant turned to the two brothers. 'Which ones are you really?'

Alistair laughed. 'For once Robert got to deal with the nonsense I usually have to put up with.'

David Bryant laughed and asked Robert, 'How does it feel to be a fox?'

'I think Alistair owes me a big favour,' Robert shuddered.

'I believe we could all use a drink and you two can tell me what you have been up to lately. Your letters, while entertaining lacked a lot of detail,' suggested Bryant.

The twins were happy to comply with his suggestion.

~~DL~~

5   Lieutenant Flinter

1804/1805

After their twenty-first birthday, Robert called in the favour in the shape of the funds for a commission as a Lieutenant in the army. Plus, the funds to purchase his uniforms and other equipment.

Robert, remembering General Bryant, wrote to him and in reply, he received a letter of introduction to the War Office. With that assistance, he purchased a commission in the Regulars and left for training. He was gone for months before he returned for leave over Christmas. He was in high spirits and excited about all he was learning. After Twelfth Night he went back to his unit for more training.

Initially, he had written a few times, and he had always been, at best, an indifferent correspondent, but the silence was now going on for too long. He had been gone for weeks without a letter, and Alistair was getting concerned.

At last, at the beginning of November, Alistair received a letter.

Somewhere in Europe, October 1805

Dear Alistair

As you can see by my direction, my training is over, and I have been deployed to the continent. I cannot, of course, tell you precisely where I am, but It is a good thing that noise does not keep me awake at night.

I am in charge of a group of good men led by a very experienced sergeant.

I say I am in charge, but truth be told, the sergeant is the one truly in charge. At least I had enough sense to listen to my superior officer, one Captain Richard Fitzwilliam, when he told me to always listen to my sergeant.

Things here are as expected. Richard was right when he told me that what he remembers most about war, are the noise and the mud. There is plenty of both.

We are holding our own, and so far, Sergeant Milton has managed to keep me out of trouble and unscathed. I pray that he continues his excellent job until I have learnt enough to return the favour.

Please do not forget to write. That is another thing I have learnt, letters from home help to keep us sane and remind us why we are doing this. I have already discovered that there is no glory in war, only necessity.

It is necessary to stop Napoleon, otherwise, the way of life that we know will disappear. And as much as I complain about many things and attitudes at home, on the whole, I like our country as it is.

It is funny, I always thought of you as the introspective one and myself as outgoing. But war and fighting do strange things to you. I find myself wondering about everything I used to take for granted.

Take, for instance, the insistence of the nobility to only marry one of 'our own'. Nobody cares about the character of their spouse, as long as they are wealthy and from the right family. In our circles, marriage is almost always a business arrangement.

In recent years I have often wondered about Aunt Francine's choice of second husband. Do not misunderstand, I like Thomas Bennet, but he is of no consequence to anyone but his family. It was not until I was here that I have come to truly realise that character is more important than any title. Now I have become convinced that Aunt has made a good choice. She picked a good and intelligent man who cares for her and their children. A title can never give as much comfort as a hug.

I just realised I have become maudlin, so I had better close for tonight, or you will think this letter is from some raving madman.

Instead of a madman, I remain your loving brother.

Robert

While grateful to have had news from Robert, Alistair now had something new to worry about. His brother's health, sanity, and life.

~~DL~~

6   Reciprocity

1806

Alistair had spent much of the previous year at the estate. Flooding had caused some problems, and he had spent months taking care of the repairs from the damage caused by the water. He had only visited town briefly to deal with his solicitors and man of business.

Now that the last of the problems was fixed, he had the opportunity to be sociable again. He had recently come back into town to renew acquaintances.

He had only just arrived at the house of Lord Sulwood, whose dinner invitation he had accepted when he ran into an old friend.

'Lord Denmere, how lovely to see you again,' Lady Alexandra gushed. 'I have not seen you in much too long. So many things have happened. You simply must call on us so that we can have a nice long chat.'

Alistair was happy to see his old friend again, but there was something in her manner that gave him pause. She was not normally this effusive.

'It would be my greatest pleasure to call on you at any time, my Lady,' he replied in the same vein. Then he asked in an undertone, 'what is wrong?'

'I will tell you all tomorrow. In the meantime, be careful of Miss Simpson,' Alexandra replied in the same way while he bowed over her hand. 'In that case, you simply must come to tea tomorrow afternoon. My aunt will be thrilled to see you again. She was saying just yesterday that it was such a shame we have not seen you lately,' she babbled on, again at full volume.

'Please give your aunt my sincerest apologies. I have not meant to neglect her, misfortunately an estate does not run itself, even with the best steward. Sometimes I have to be there to look after business.' He tried to look contrite.

'That is all men ever seem to think about,' she pouted, 'business.'

'But it keeps the ladies in our lives in silks and jewels,' teased Alistair.

'You do not have a lady in your life,' retorted Lady Alexandra.

'Not yet. But one day I will have, and she will be just as demanding as all the other ladies of the ton.' Alistair smiled teasingly at his friend. 'If I spend the time now to provide for the future, I will have more time to spend with the lady once I am married, which will prevent her from scolding me for neglecting her.'

'For the sake of a lady, you have not even met yet, you make all of us suffer,' pouted Alexandra. 'You shall make it up to my Aunt and myself tomorrow.'

'It will be my pleasure,' Alistair assured her.

'Ah, there you are Lord Denmere. I am thrilled that you accepted my husband's invitation,' gushed Lady Sulwood. 'Have you met all our other guests? No? Let me introduce you. We should have a charming evening. We have such diverse guests.' His hostess proceeded to suit her actions to her words.

When everyone went in to dinner, Alistair found that Miss Simpson had been placed next to him at the table. Lady Alexandra was seated opposite him.

During dinner, Alistair tried to draw out Miss Simpson about her interests. It appeared that all she was interested in was fashion and her accomplishments, which she appeared to have learnt by rote.

When the ladies rose to retire to the drawing-room, Miss Simpson was a little slow to leave since, apparently, her reticule had become caught in the lace of her gown. The port had been poured by the time she untangled it. She became so flustered that she dropped the reticule as she rose to leave.

Alistair, ever the gentleman, bent to pick it up for her. Just as he was trying to hand the object to its owner, Lady Alexandra stumbled as she walked past him. Her reflexive grasp to catch herself from falling, jostled his arm, which in turn sent the reticule on a collision course with his glass of port.

Lady Alexandra was mortified. 'Lord Denmere, Lord Sulwood, I must apologise for my clumsiness. Maybe the wine was a little strong for me. I am not normally so unsteady.'

'No harm done, my Lady. There is nothing broken, and there is plenty more port,' Lord Sulwood assured her.

'You are too kind, my Lord.' She raised a hand to her forehead. 'I believe a cup of coffee with the ladies will set me right. Miss Simpson, shall we join the ladies?' She politely asked the other lady, who had again taken possession of her reticule. She then took Miss Simpson's arm and led the lady out of the dining room.

~~DL~~

At two o'clock the following afternoon, Alistair presented himself at Hunter House. He was shown into the family parlour, where he was greeted by the Countess of Marven and Lady Alexandra.

Both appeared anxious to see him. 'I hope nothing untoward has befallen you since last night?' asked the Countess.

'I am perfectly well. What is this all about? Why are you so anxious?' Alistair was puzzled.

Both ladies smiled in relief. Lady Beatrice responded, 'Alexandra overheard a conversation to the effect that Miss Simpson is trying to compromise you. We had heard that she was to be at the dinner last night. Alexandra managed to get herself invited to give you warning.'

'But I could not go into detail while there was a chance we might be overheard.'

'Can you give me the details now? Miss Simpson seemed quite harmless when I met her last night. She is not a lady I could ever be interested in, but she did not seem desperate enough to force a compromise.'

'The day before yesterday I was at Almack's. While I was in the lady's retiring room, I was sitting down and fixing one of my shoe roses, when two ladies came into the room. Since it was not obvious that I was present, they discussed a plan of putting a sleeping draught into your

30

port and then placing you into bed with Miss Simpson. Unfortunately, I do not know where or when,' Lady Alexandra explained.

'I was rather concerned that when we were getting up to move to the drawing-room. Her hand was very close to your glass.'

'Was that why you jostled my elbow and made me spill it?' Alistair asked concerned. 'I know that you are not usually so clumsy or prone to fainting.'

'I am more prone to feinting of a different kind.' Alexandra grinned. 'Although I am not certain that it was necessary under the circumstances, I did not wish to take a chance. She may try elsewhere.'

'I would assume it would be at a private function,' Alistair mused. 'Otherwise, they will not have access to a bedroom. Do you know where she is staying? She mentioned last night that she was only visiting London.'

'I heard her mention a Cousin George, but I do not have a surname,' Alexandra replied.

'Maybe for the foreseeable future, I should not accept invitations by anybody named George until we find out where she is staying. But why did you not simply send a note?'

'As you well know, ladies are not supposed to correspond with men to whom they are not engaged, and Aunt Beatrice was out. It was also somewhat nebulous, and I truly did not wish to put that sort of information into a letter.'

She now grinned, 'although I was quite prepared to make a scene if you did not leave on your own feet last night.'

'I appreciate your concern, but I would not want to place you in an untenable position. And although I like you well enough, I do not wish to marry you.'

'Ever the charming gentleman,' Lady Beatrice teased.

'You know perfectly well that I think of you as two of my best friends. I simply have no wish to marry a friend, who is only a friend. And you never know, one of these days Alexandra might meet someone whom she wishes to marry. It would be a shame if she were shackled in a marriage already.'

'Aunt, you know well enough that the feeling is mutual as far as Alistair is concerned. I have someone else in mind.'

'You do? Who is the lucky man and when should I congratulate you?' Alister asked with a relieved grin.

'His name is irrelevant since he does not yet know. He is proving rather myopic.' Lady Alexandra shrugged. 'But there is no hurry for me. You, on the other hand, need to ensure that you are on your guard. It is a pity that Robert is away again. He makes such a wonderful decoy.'

Lady Beatrice chimed in, 'ladies are rarely interested in younger sons. Especially when they appear not to have a title or fortune.'

'Robert is very happy that the family decided on keeping his prospects very quiet. I only wish I had had the same opportunity,' sighed Alistair.

'It must be terrible to be so very desirable,' teased Lady Beatrice. 'Console yourself, it's a Duke's life, but someone has to do it.'

~~DL~~

'Lord Denmere, you have been very elusive lately,' remarked Lady Beatrice when Alistair called on the lady the next time. 'We have not seen you in weeks.'

'I am sorry, my Lady, some business matters at the estate needed my immediate attention. But I have returned to bask in the pleasure of your company,' he replied effusively with a mischievous smile.

'You are a scamp and a rogue,' chided the Countess, 'but since you are so very charming about it, I will forgive you.'

'Have you been keeping well in my absence, my Lady?'

'Tolerably well, thank you. Unfortunately, my age is starting to creep up on me.' Lady Beatrice sighed theatrically. 'I suppose it happens to all of us eventually.'

'You could never age, my Lady. You are as beautiful and charming as ever,' Alistair flirted outrageously.

'Behave yourself or I will have Alexandra to have words with you,' threatened the lady laughingly.

'Speaking of your niece, I hope she is well?' Alistair had noted the absence of his friend.

'She is very well indeed. She is visiting with friends in the country,' the countess answered the implied question. 'I expect her back in a few weeks.'

'I shall look forward to seeing her then,' said Alistair a little disappointed. Although he had no matrimonial interest in Lady Alexandra, she was a good friend whose company and conversation he enjoyed.

'Since you have been out of town, you may not have heard the latest on dit about a mutual acquaintance,' smirked Lady Beatrice. 'I know that you do not usually listen to gossip, so the chances are that you have not heard that a young lady of your acquaintance has landed herself in a predicament.'

'Since you find it amusing, it must be someone of whom you are not overly fond,' postulated Alistair.

'You are correct, although I have not met the young lady, my niece is acquainted with her, as are you.' She smiled mischievously.

'It appears that when Miss Simpson became tired of waiting for a chance at you, she chose another quarry. The gentleman in question did not even need much persuasion to sample her charms,' the Countess related the tale with a certain relish. 'Unfortunately for her, when she cried compromise, he laughed at her. She is only lucky that he has no interest in spreading the story beyond his own circle.'

'Does that mean it is safe for me to go out into society again? If Miss Simpson thinks her reputation safe, she may try again.' Alistair wondered.

Now the Countess looked a little uncertain. 'You are perfectly safe.' After a moment's thought, she appeared to come to a decision. 'I was not certain if I should tell you who the gentleman in question is. But the reason *you* are safe is that Miss Simpson would assume your father would not allow her to marry you.'

'Are you saying she tried to compromise the Duke of Denton?' Alistair was flabbergasted.

'It seems she thought that if she could not be your wife, she would be your mother,' the lady explained.

Alistair could not help himself, he laughed uproariously. 'Oh dear, she certainly picked the wrong man.'

'Yes, it is terrible, is it not?' Lady Beatrice said with mock sympathy.

~~DL~~

7   Love Hurts

1808

The Season in London is such fun Lord Denmere thought sarcastically when he attended yet another ball.

The elegant ladies dressed in the latest fashions... and only one in one hundred could look elegant in those fashions.

The incredible variety of perfumes... too liberally applied to cover the fact that the person had not bathed in a month.

The ostentatious display of jewels... either too gaudy or paste because the originals were sold to cover gambling debts – the so-called debts of honour. Although Alistair could never understand what was honourable about gambling too much.

The stimulating conversation... about the weather.

The exciting exchange of information... the latest on dit about everyone's newest paramour.

Oh, yes. What a thrilling experience. Alistair attended because, at the age of five and twenty, he felt duty-bound to start looking for a wife.

His grandmother had suggested he should start looking at the available candidates. She was not pushing him to marry but asked him to keep an open mind. His desire to please his grandmother combined with his sense of duty to produce an heir.

Now he stood at the side of the ballroom bored witless, suffocating in the stifling room. To add injury to insult, his feet ached from dancing, and the stifling air gave him a headache.

He was just preparing to leave, even though the hour was still early when his attention was captured by an amusing sight.

Across the room, he spotted Fitzwilliam Darcy looking like he had bitten into a lemon. On his right side stood that puppy Bingley, who slavishly followed Darcy whenever he had the chance. Bingley was beaming good-humouredly while he apparently chattered away at Darcy.

On Darcy's left was the probable cause of his sour looks. Bingley's younger sister, Miss Caroline, was hanging off Darcy's arm. She appeared to have a death-grip, which nothing short of amputation was going to release.

Alistair was amazed that the friendship between those two men, which had started almost six years ago at Cambridge, still survived.

He supposed that Bingley's easy manners helped Darcy to navigate the shark-infested waters of London society. Although now there was a price attached to that assistance. Or in this case to his arm.

No matter, whatever the case, Alistair decided, it was Darcy's problem.

~~DL~~

Alistair turned to leave when he saw... her.

He thought she must be Helen of Troy. The face that launched a thousand ships or possibly a thousand hearts. His own heart was certainly pounding at the sight.

She was perfection. From her raven hair to her dancing slippers, she was a vision from the fertile imagination of an artist. No flesh and blood human could be so perfect.

Needless to say, Alistair was smitten.

'She is quite a beauty, do you not agree?' a voice next to him awoke him to his surroundings. He looked at the speaker and recognised his mentor.

'Mr Bryant, how wonderful to see you. I did not know you were in town,' Alistair exclaimed.

'I had some business with required my urgent attention. Fortunately, it did not take long to conclude, so I decided to accept the invitation to tonight's ball. It is good to see you looking so well,' David Bryant said with a genuine smile for his young friend.

'Will you be staying long? I hope you will have time to dine with us one evening.'

'I will be here for a few days, and I would be delighted to catch up with you and Her Grace' was the happy response. 'But I noticed you looking at Lady Francesca. From the look on your face, I gather you have not met her before.'

'She is real flesh and blood then? I thought her to be a vision,' Alistair admitted.

'She is real, and in the short time she has been out in society, she has cut quite a swathe through the hearts of all the young and not so young men in town.'

'How do you know all this if you only just arrived in town?' Alistair was puzzled.

'I am staying at my club. Most people think that women are the worst gossips. They have obviously never been in a gentleman's club when the gentlemen are half cut. As long as there are no women around to hear, men are worse gossips than women ever will be. Of course, they call it exchanging information. But a rose by any other name...' Bryant smiled sarcastically.

'Have you made her acquaintance?' Alistair asked hopefully.

'I have, and she gave me barely any notice. I suppose my position, wealth and looks are too far beneath her aim. If you wish, I can introduce you, but I must caution you that the lady appears ambitious, to put it politely,' Bryant advised his friend.

'I would say with her looks she is in a position to choose whomever she wants. But I venture to postulate that if a lady has a choice between an old husband and a young, personable one, it would be easier to fall in love with the latter. Especially if all other factors are the same.' Alistair was not so easily put off. 'So, if you would be so kind as to introduce us, I would like the opportunity to make my case to the lady.'

'If that is your wish, come with me. But guard your heart,' Bryant cautioned again before leading Alistair towards the lady.

'Lady Francesca, my friend asked for the honour of an introduction.'

When the lady said, 'I would be delighted,' Bryant said, 'Lord Denmere, I would like to make known to you Lady Francesca deMille.

Lady Francesca, I have the honour of introducing to you Alistair Flinter, Marquess of Denmere.'

'I am most pleased to meet you, Lord Denmere,' Lady Francesca said while offering her hand.

'I am enchanted to make your acquaintance, Lady Francesca,' Alistair said, bowing over the lady's hand.

When he straightened up again, Alistair asked, 'may I be so bold as to enquire if perchance you have any dances available?'

'You are in luck, Lord Denmere. I have the second last set still free.' The Lady smiled charmingly at him.

'In that case, my Lady, may I claim that set?'

'You may, Lord Denmere, and I shall anticipate it with the greatest of pleasure.'

'But the set now starting is mine, my Lady,' said one of her companions with a proprietary smile while offering his arm.

'It is indeed, Your Grace.' Lady Francesca smiled as she took the proffered arm. 'If you will excuse us,' she offered to the rest of the company as she was being led to the dancefloor.

~~DL~~

Since Alistair was now bound to wait for the second last set, he escaped to the balcony for a breath of fresh air to try and ease his pounding head.

As he stepped into the darkest corner to escape the notice of the other guests, he realised that the corner was already occupied by none other than Fitzwilliam Darcy.

'Good evening, Darcy. Are you hiding from Miss Bingley?' he teased the other man.

Darcy looked uncomfortable. 'You sound like my cousin Richard,' he said without actually answering Alistair's question.

'That is high praise indeed,' joked Alistair, who was already starting to recover in the cool and fresh air.

'Ah, yes. I forgot that you and your brother spent two years in his company at Cambridge.'

'Those were fun years.' Alistair could not resist trying to shake Darcy out of his reserve. 'But the most astonishing part was that we actually learned.'

That raised a small smile on Darcy's face, and he unbent enough that they managed a pleasant conversation about mutual acquaintances from Cambridge.

Eventually, it was time for Alistair to claim his dances with Lady Francesca.

~~DL~~

The next few weeks were hectic for Alistair, who normally kept a much lower profile in society.

He did not get to spend as much time as he wished to in company of the lady, but he took every opportunity he could get.

The more he was able to converse with her, the higher his opinion became of Lady Francesca.

Due to the fact that they never had the chance to speak in true privacy, they had to stick to innocuous topics. In the lady's favour was the fact that she was intelligent and enjoyed reading. She was even able to discuss history and politics.

He was now completely lost. For the first time in his life, he considered matrimony with something other than revulsion. He only hoped that he could be worthy of such an exquisite lady.

~~DL~~

Since Alistair was too early for his call on Lady Francesca, he decided to stroll in the garden of her uncle's house. He could just as easily have strolled in the garden of Denton House, but he wanted to be as close as possible to the lady who had completely bewitched him.

He did not pay any attention to his surroundings since his mind was fully occupied with visions of Lady Francesca's perfect features, pleasing figure and memories of how her light touch on his arm had roused his passions. Alistair admitted to himself that he was head over heels in love with the lady. He was so absorbed in his fond imaginings that, when he heard her voice, he thought it part of his memories until another voice cut in.

'Have you decided yet which of your suitors you are going to reel in?' he heard a vaguely familiar feminine voice ask.

'Not yet. The choice is between the Duke, the Marquess and the Earl.' He was shocked when he realised this voice came from the lips of Lady Francesca, although the tone was considerably colder than was her wont. His concern about who the other woman was, went immediately out of his mind. The only thing that mattered was what the woman he loved had to say.

'Which one do you favour?'

'The Duke has the position and the wealth I like. Since he is middle-aged and not particularly attractive, his demands on me should not be so great, and once I am with child, I can probably steer him back to his mistress. Once the child is born, I can introduce Patrick to the household to keep me amused.'

Alistair was stunned to hear her considering the Duke in those terms. And who the devil was Patrick?

'The Marquess, on the other hand, is young and good looking, and he will be a Duke one day. Therefore, he also has the station and the wealth. But I believe he likes living in the country rather than town and I definitely prefer the town. It is also doubtful whether I can fob him off on a mistress and I do not wish to give up Patrick.'

Could she be speaking of himself? It was true he preferred living in the country, but he did not have a mistress and had no intention of ever having one.

'Since you want to continue with him as your lover, why do you not simply marry Patrick?' asked her friend.

'Are you out of your mind. He is poor. All he has is five hundred pound a year. You do not really expect me to live on *that*,' Francesca sounded outraged.

Alistair was outraged too. But for a different reason. This woman, he could no longer think of her as a lady, was completely mercenary and apparently without morals.

'You do have expensive tastes. I suppose you will have to marry one of your noblemen. What about the Earl?'

'In some respects, he would be the best option. He is older than the others and is mainly interested in a young wife to show off. Since he has grown children, he will not expect me to produce an heir, which will be a relief. Given a choice, I would rather not risk childbirth. Too many women die. But best of all, he is the richest of the three, *and* he likes living in town.'

'How does Patrick feel about being your lover rather than your husband?'

'He is so besotted with me he will agree to any arrangement as long as he can continue to have me,' Francesca gloated.

'Continue? Are you not afraid you could end up with child before you hook your husband? Men tend to be quite particular about these kinds of details.'

'I would have you know, I am still a virgin.' Francesca laughed. 'As long as you are not missish, there are a lot of ways you both can have fun. And there is not the slightest risk of pregnancy,' she sounded quite proud of herself.

~~DL~~

Alistair had heard enough. He had thought Francesca cared for him. Maybe not as much as he loved her, but cared for him, nonetheless.

But she was cold and calculating. He could accept a certain amount of calculation. After all, most marriages amongst the members of the *ton* were business arrangements. But to the best of his knowledge, they did not normally evaluate a potential husband by how easy he would be to cuckold. At least he hoped not.

But it hurt abominably that he had been fooled into believing the lady reciprocated his feelings.

He returned to Denton House in a black humour. On arrival, he went straight away to his suite and ordered a bottle of brandy to be brought to him.

He proceeded to get drunk.

~~DL~~

Alistair woke with a pounding headache, but with a much clearer mind than he had had the night before.

While getting drunk, he had considered many possibilities. One of which was to get revenge on the lady for toying with his heart by exposing her lover.

He now realised he had offered her his heart to play with. It was not her doing that broke it. He had deluded himself into thinking she cared for him. He also realised that most of the pain he felt was due to injured pride rather than a broken heart.

Revenge would hurt him more than her. Yes, he could ruin her life by exposing her plans but what kind of a man would that make him?

He decided that was not the kind of man that he wanted to be.

It also made him think of the kind of woman he wanted for a wife. With Lady Francesca, he had always been on his best behaviour because he was trying to impress her.

He now knew he needed a lady with whom he could be himself. Someone he could like and respect, and someone who would like and respect him in return.

Lady Alexandra had had the right of it. Character was important. All else was window dressing.

Alistair, Marquess of Denmere was starting to grow up. It was quite a heady feeling.

~~DL~~

The Dowager was perplexed when Alistair stayed home all day without fidgeting. Eventually, her curiosity overcame her determination not to meddle in his affairs.

'Are you not going to call on Lady Francesca today?' she asked.

'No, grandmother, I will not.' After a moment's hesitation, he added, 'I am only planning on seeing her one more time. To take my leave when I return to the estate.'

'I see. Has something happened that changed your mind about the lady? Just yesterday you were eager for her company.' The Dowager was relieved to hear that he seemed to have lost interest in Lady Francesca. She felt that her grandson deserved better than an ambitious and cold-hearted social climber.

'I have discovered something about the lady's character, which makes me doubt her fitness to be my wife, even if she had any interest in me, which I believe is not the case.' Alistair tried to be casual. Even though he had determined that she was mercenary, it still hurt that she would prefer an old Earl over himself. But he reassured himself, that was hurt pride speaking, not a hurt heart.

'While I am sorry that the situation did not work out for you, I am happy because I think you can do much better than a woman with a pretty face but no character.' When she noticed Alistair's startled look, she added, 'I was not blinded by her beauty.'

'Thank you for not interfering. I appreciate your trust in me.'

'You are a grown man. You have to make your own decisions. I also felt that sooner or later, she would show her true character to you. What are your plans now?'

'I think I will go back to the estate and oversee the spring planting. After that, who knows.' Alistair found a genuine smile for the woman who cared about him so greatly.

~~DL~~

He called on Lady Francesca one final time.

Several other visitors were present, mostly gentlemen who were calling on the beautiful woman. Alistair noticed that all of the visitors were young, and he wondered if her other suitors would call at different times or if they had also seen the light.

Lady Francesca gushed, 'I have not seen you in several days, Lord Denmere. I was afraid you had deserted me.'

'I am sorry, my Lady, but I received some information that I had to deal with urgently,' he shrugged deprecatingly while he gave her his most charming smile.

'But you are here now, and I hope you will have time to join us for dinner tomorrow.' Lady Francesca gave him her best alluring smile. Since she had seen him last, her two other candidates seemed to have deserted her for other ladies. Now the Marquess was the best of her admirers, and she was determined to reel him in.

Alistair smiled sadly. 'I am sorry I will not be able to enjoy your charming company. I am devastated, but estate business calls me away. I am afraid it will probably be months before I will have a chance to return to London and your charming society. By which time I expect you will have given your heart to someone who can give you the attention you deserve.'

Alistair was very proud of himself. He spoke nothing but the truth, but the meaning was very different from what the lady heard.

After some more polite conversation, he stood to make his farewells.

'I am afraid I must take my leave of you,' he said as he took her proffered hand.

'I hope you and Master Patrick will be very happy together,' he murmured in a low voice as he bowed over her hand.

He had the satisfaction of hearing her gasp. When he straightened up, her face betrayed no emotion, but her eyes held fear.

Alistair smiled pleasantly as he released her hand. 'Goodbye, Lady Francesca,' he said and with a polite nod turned away and left the room, the house, and her life.

~~DL~~

8   London Season

1809

Major Robert Flinter and his fellow officers who had also been assigned to the War Office, attended one of the finest balls of the season. He had arrived in London only that afternoon and had barely had time to get cleaned up and changed into his best uniform, before being whisked off to join the revelry.

He was still recuperating from wounds received in a skirmish in the previous autumn. The other result of the skirmish was his promotion to Brevet Major. That had come as a surprise since he had been a Captain for only three years. He felt that during that time, the only thing that distinguished him was his ability to keep most of his men alive while still achieving his missions. It appeared his superiors thought this an achievement worthy of promotion.

He hoped to encounter most of his family at the ball, with the exception of his brother who had again retreated to the country. From hints in Alistair's letters, Robert assumed that his brother was either nursing a broken heart or shattered illusions, or possibly both. Lady Francesca must have been exceptional, both in her ability to turn his brother's head and her ambitions.

The shattered illusions surprised Robert since both he and Alistair were aware how the ton operated. Wealth, position, and reputation was everything to most of them.

Now he was curious to see how his cousins were handling the London Season. His grandmother's letters had included a comment that both Elizabeth and Jane were to have their presentations. Elizabeth's lack of patience with either flattery or arrogance should be amusing to watch.

~~DL~~

They had been at the ball for only a few minutes and were standing in a group admiring the latest crop of debutants, who were vying for attention.

As Robert looked around, he spotted three Ladies strolling toward the refreshment table. He immediately recognised his aunt and his cousin Elizabeth. They were in company of Lady Sefton, whom he vaguely remembered being introduced to at another function.

When they spotted him, the ladies changed direction toward him. He realised there was some deception being played out, when Lady Sefton, the consummate society matron, immediately made the 'introductions'. 'Lady Francine, do you remember Major Flinter?'

'Yes, of course, I remember being introduced to the gentleman. Although at the time he was only a Lieutenant.' Turning to Robert, she said, 'congratulations on your promotion, Major. Do you remember my daughter, Lady Elizabeth?'

'It is wonderful to see you again in society, Lady Francine, and of course, I remember Lady Elizabeth. How could I forget so charming a lady?' Robert smiled his most charming smile. 'Might I have the pleasure of the first set with you, Lady Elizabeth? That is of course if I am not too late, and you are already engaged?' He bowed to Elizabeth.

'You are in luck, Major. We are only just arrived, and you are the first gentleman with whom we have spoken; therefore, I have the set available,' Elizabeth informed her cousin while maintaining her polite smile, rather than allowing her impish grin to surface.

'You have made me the happiest of men, Lady Elizabeth,' he responded. He then turned to his fellow officers and declared with a grin, 'I am certain you will excuse me to much more charming company than yourselves.'

The officers naturally agreed, although chagrined that Robert should immediately upon arrival find such lovely company.

Lady Sefton drifted away from the group, while Lady Francine led the way to a quiet spot at the side of the room, before turning to her nephew. 'Robert, what are you doing in town. I had no idea you would be present.'

'A group of us have just been temporarily posted to the War Office. We only arrived today. I had heard from grandmother that you would attend the season, and since we received an invitation to this ball, I was hoping to meet you here. I assumed, correctly as it seems, that you would be here, rather than at Denton House.'

'I am exceedingly happy to see you, apart from having you partner Elizabeth, I am pleased to see you apparently well.' Lady Francine turned the last part into a question.

'Yes, I am well. I had a bit of a scrape late last year, but it is all healed up,' he reassured his aunt. 'Are you here alone, or is anyone else from the family present?'

'Mother is here with Jane and her father. I am certain Jane will be happy to have a congenial dance partner if you are so inclined.'

'I will make a point of it. If Jane has grown into the beauty she promised to be when I last saw her, I shall be the envy of all my fellow officers,' Robert agreed.

~~DL~~

Elizabeth and Robert lined up for the first set with the other dancers. They made a rather stunning looking couple. He in his red regimentals and she in a white gown with a subtle pattern of green vines embroidered on all the hems.

They could see Jane across the room, in a dress similar to Elizabeth's but with small blue flowers instead of the vines and a few more flowers scattered on the bodice. She also looked exquisite, and her dance partner obviously appreciated her beauty. Even Robert could tell that Jane thought the gentleman's admiration was rather too obvious.

Elizabeth confirmed this when she suggested, 'Robert, please make certain you dance the next set with Jane. That man,' she indicated Jane's current partner with a look in his direction, 'is much too familiar for her comfort.'

'I will make a point of dissuading anyone who might have the wrong ideas or intentions.' Robert reassured Lizzy.

For the next set, he made good his promise, much to Jane's relief.

'I can now understand mother's attitude to the *ton.* I am only grateful that we have already decided this will be the last ball we attend unless something changes drastically.'

'Seeing all the manoeuvring going on, I am grateful to be a second son,' Robert commented. 'I can attend a ball for the fun of dancing, but nobody has a serious interest in me.'

~~DL~~

Robert's reprieve in London did not last long. In April he was back in Portugal.

Alistair had become resigned to the intermittent correspondence from his brother. Eventually, another letter arrived.

Somewhere on the Iberian Peninsula, 21st August, 1809

Dear Alistair

This is just a quick note to assure you that I am well.

It was an interesting campaign, but the threat of reinforcements of the opposition and lack of supplies forced us to retreat to our current location.

Sergeant Milton was injured but is recovering well, although it is uncertain if he will be fit for duty again. If he does not regain full use of his leg, I hope you will find him a position at Denton. He is intelligent and excellent at handling men.

My new rank is now permanent.

If all goes well, I will be home for Christmas. You had best get an extra boiler. I will want at least one hot bath every single day.

Your dirty but safe brother

Robert

~~DL~~

9   Duke of Denton

1810

When Major Robert Flinter arrived back in England late in November, he sent a note to his grandmother informing her of his return.

Her reply made him hurry to London.

When he arrived at Denton House, he was surprised to find the Dowager in relatively good spirits.

'Good afternoon, grandmother,' He greeted the Dowager.

'Robert,' she beamed at him, 'it is so very good to see you. I hope you are well?'

'Considering I survived another year on the continent, I am in remarkably fine fettle. I was concerned about you though when you sent word that your son had died,' replied Robert, who refused to acknowledge that the Dowager's son had been his father.

'There is no need to worry about me. I lost my first son, your name's sake Robert, the year you were born. That hurt abominably because he loved life, and he had his life cut short.'

She sighed and continued with a sad little smile, 'your father effectively died the same year. His body survived all these years, but his spirit died with your mother's passing. I mourned both my sons then. Now I just feel a sense of relief. How do you feel?'

'I feel happy to see you, and I look forward to spending Christmas with you and Alistair in a building where the roof does not leak, and the food is not only edible but tastes good. In the meantime, I am happy to help you in any way that I can. As long as you do not expect me to grieve over a man I have never known.'

'I have already made all the arrangements to have Alexander's body removed to Denton Manor so that he can be buried in the family crypt. I have also informed his solicitors who will make all the legal arrangements to have the title transferred to Alistair,' explained the Dowager. 'I will travel to Denton Manor with the body, and I would appreciate your company.'

'I wish to go home for Christmas and having your company on the way will make the journey much more pleasurable.' Robert smiled fondly at his grandmother.

He was surprised when suddenly her face lit up with her old impish smile. 'I suspect you will be even more grateful for my company when you can use me as an excuse to avoid all those eager young ladies who will wish to know you, intimately.'

'Why would young ladies wish to know me, intimately or even otherwise?' Robert was puzzled.

'Have you forgotten how popular Alistair has always been with the ladies?' his grandmother queried.

'How can I forget all those simpering fools who kept throwing themselves at Alistair, because he is a Marquess. But what has that to do with me?'

'Alistair is now Duke, and he is unmarried and does not have a son. Can you tell me who the current heir apparent is?' the Dowager now sported a full-blown grin.

Robert suddenly realised the point the Dowager was making. 'Oh no. I have no wish to be a Duke. Or even a Marquess. I do not wish to be the target of every matchmaker in town.'

'In that case, you are lucky to be in mourning and leaving for the country in the morning. Do you not agree?'

~~DL~~

Alistair received a black-edged letter addressed to Alistair, the Duke of Denton. The handwriting was his grandmother's.

He was grateful that the title on the envelope gave him the message before even opening the letter. A black-edged letter would have made him fear the worst for his brother otherwise.

The message, when he opened the letter, was brief and to the point. It also contained excellent news for him.

Dear Alistair

I wanted to be the one to inform you that your father passed away last night of winter fever.

There is no need to trouble yourself with coming to London. I will escort Alexander's body to Denton Manor for burial in the family crypt.

Your brother Robert has just arrived back in town and will accompany me on the journey.

Please arrange with the rector to conduct a funeral service on Thursday.

The solicitors will be in touch with you soon to transfer the title to you.

I will see you soon, and in the meantime remain

Your loving grandmother.

~~DL~~

Late on Tuesday afternoon, a convoy of three carriages arrived at Denton Manor. The Dowager, Major Robert Flinter and the Dowager's companion, Anne Hopkins, occupied the first and most comfortable carriage. The body of Alexander, the former Duke of Denton, was carried in the second, while their luggage and servants brought up the rear.

Alistair, who was expecting them, stood ready to greet his grandmother and his brother. 'Grandmother, I am sorry for your loss,' he said after he handed the Dowager from the carriage.

'Thank you, Alistair,' she replied.

'Your Grace, it is wonderful to see you,' Robert said with a bow and a grin for his brother.

'Not you too,' groaned Alistair. 'I have been graced to death for the last two days already.'

'You had better get used to it, Your Grace,' added a smiling Mrs Hopkins, who had been handed out of the carriage by Robert.

'I am happy to see all of you, but shall we go inside where it is warmer?' Alistair suggested.

As they entered the manor, Robert said, 'I am looking forward to a hot bath.'

'You kept the servants running, providing you with baths while we were at Denton House, do you not think you are clean enough?' laughed the Dowager.

'Grandmother, after the year I have had, hot baths are the greatest luxury of civilised living,' protested Robert.

'Mrs Carter,' Alistair called out to the housekeeper who was hovering in the background. 'I hope the new boiler I asked you to arrange for has been fired up. While my brother is here, please, ensure that hot baths are ready for him at any time, day or night. We must demonstrate our thanks for his defence of our country and our way of life.' His smile, more than his words, showed his care for his brother.

~~DL~~

The body of Alexander, the late Duke of Denton, was placed in the chapel at Denton Manor.

There he lay in state until he was laid to rest in the family crypt, next to his beloved wife Lady Penelope.

The brothers attended the funeral out of a sense of duty and respect for the family name.

The Dowagers had said her farewells to her son privately before the official mourners arrived.

~~DL~~

10 Return to Denton House

1812

Alistair, Duke of Denton, had spent an enjoyable year predominantly at his home estate. His excuse, that he was in mourning for his father, was just that, an excuse. But it had made the year a pleasure.

It had kept the matchmakers at bay as well as any other unwanted company.

Not that he objected to company, he simply was selective in the company he did enjoy.

Now he was back in London at his father's townhouse.

He had visited it briefly, shortly after his father's death, to arrange for a skeleton staff to maintain the house and to reassign the excess staff. He had been horrified at the taste, or lack thereof, in which the house was furnished. He had decided that the house needed to be redecorated.

Since his arrival, he inspected the whole house and could not find a single bedchamber that he was prepared to use.

He turned to his valet, Parker, who was waiting patiently to unpack his trunks, 'Please have my trunks loaded onto the carriage again. I think I need to impose on Her Grace. These rooms are just too much...'

'Thank you, Your Grace. I am grateful to be staying at Denton House,' Parker replied with a suppressed sigh of relief.

~~DL~~

The butler, Barton, announced 'His Grace, the Duke of Denton' just before Alistair strode into the room.

He bowed to the Dowager. 'Forgive my intrusion grandmother. I did not know you had company.'

'You are forgiven Alistair since your timing is perfect. You can take your aunt and cousin to the theatre tomorrow night.'

Alistair turned to the other ladies in the room. 'Aunt, you look as lovely as ever. If you were not already married, I would try to sweep you off your feet,' he flirted shamelessly.

'And you are still a charming rogue, nephew,' responded Mrs Bennet.

He then turned to Elizabeth 'I was not aware I had such a ravishingly beautiful cousin. The only grown-up cousin I know of is a very impertinent little hoyden, whose aim with a snowball is wickedly accurate. You cannot possibly be her.' He grinned at Lizzy.

'I think you are now an even worse tease than you were in the past, but I am happy to see you again nonetheless.'

He walked over to her and bowed over her hand. 'Seriously though, you are remarkably improved. I will be the envy of all the men at the theatre.'

'Wait till you see Jane, then you will know what real beauty is. She has grown up too, in the years since you last saw her.' She laughed. Secretly though she was flattered. Despite Alistair's flirtatious and light-hearted manner, she knew he was not given to insincere flattery.

The Dowager explained to her grandson 'You will of course act with the utmost propriety and not mention your familial relationships.'

'Are you still dodging fortune hunters, Aunt?' he asked with a grin. 'It will be my pleasure to pull the wool over the eyes of the unperceptive.'

Mrs Bennet quietly said to her mother, 'Mama, you would put Machiavelli to shame.'

'I am glad you appreciate my talents,' the old lady responded with a twinkle in her eyes.

Turning back to her grandson, she asked. 'Now that we have the important things taken care of, what brings you to my house?'

'Since I am now out of mourning for my dear unlamented father, I thought I would redecorate the townhouse. His tastes were somewhat more, shall we say ornate, than mine.'

'No, we shall be truthful and say ostentatious, pretentious as well as lascivious. Knowing you, I did not think you would want to live in a house reminiscent of a bordello.'

Lizzy gasped at her grandmother's words. Mrs Bennet just looked sad at the reminder that her brother had turned out in a similar mould as her father.

Alistair chided, 'you have upset Cousin Lizzy.'

'Sorry, dear. I forgot that you were raised with much better manners and values than most of the ton. Anyway, Alistair, to get back to the point, why are you here?'

'I was going to stay at the house to direct the redecorating, but I could not stomach the current decoration, so I was hoping to beg a bed of you. I did not, of course, know you already had houseguests. Otherwise, I would not have considered to impose on you.'

'Nonsense, it is no imposition. I enjoy having my family here for a change. I am certain Barton will be able to find you a cupboard somewhere where you can hang your hat.'

She rang the bell. When the butler entered, she directed, 'Barton, find a room for his Grace. He will be staying here for a few weeks.'

Barton suggested, 'the blue suite?'

'Yes, that seems like an adequate cupboard for your hat.'

~~DL~~

The suite to which Barton led him was more than adequate 'to hang his hat'. In fact, it was almost the equivalent to the Master suite which he now occupied at Denton Manor. Except this suite had the advantage that the Dowager's taste was obvious in the decoration.

Parker, who had followed him, sighed with pleasure. 'This is much more the thing, Your Grace.'

Barton turned to Parker, explaining, 'there is a small bedchamber past the dressing room which you may use, Mr Parker.'

'Thank you, Mr Barton. If you could have our luggage brought up, I would be most obliged.'

'It has already been arranged. Hot water for a bath will be brought up shortly. Is there anything else you require, Your Grace?' Barton asked in an almost reverent tone which he usually reserved for the Dowager.

'Not at the moment, thank you, Barton.' Alistair dismissed the butler.

'It appears we both have moved up in the world,' quipped Parker. When Alistair cocked a questioning eyebrow, Parker elaborated. 'Mr Barton never before called me Mister.'

'Just be sure not to let it go to your head, or you might need some new hats. And I am not certain this cupboard has enough room for them,' Alistair said with a grin.

~~DL~~

After dinner, Alistair was comfortably ensconced in the library with a book and a glass of brandy, when his cousin entered the room.

'Hello, Alistair. I thought you had gone to bed,' said Elizabeth as she went to a bookcase to find some reading material for herself.

'I am tired, but I am also not ready to go to sleep, so I came to my favourite room.' Alistair smiled at his cousin, 'I see you still love to read as well.'

'I do, and grandmother has a wonderful collection. I take advantage of it every time I am in town.'

'Would you forgo reading for a while and keep me company? I would like to ask you something.'

'That sounds ominous,' Elizabeth teased but moved to take a chair near her cousin. 'What can I do to enlighten you?'

'I am curious why I am taking you to the theatre. Do not misunderstand, I am delighted to accompany you and Aunt Francine, but I suspect there is more to this outing than just to enjoy a play.'

'I think grandmother is hoping that word of me being seen with you will get back to someone we know.' Elizabeth blushed and looked down at her hands.

'Now I am truly curious. Do your blushes mean that there is a gentleman involved?' Alistair teased. When Elizabeth nodded, he asked gently, 'will you tell me the full story?'

'It involves Mr Darcy of Derbyshire,' Lizzy started.

'Dutiful Darcy, the wet blanket is making my cousin blush,' Alistair was astonished.

'He can be quite charming. He is also intelligent and a wonderful conversationalist,' Elizabeth heatedly defended Darcy.

'I beg your pardon. I had not meant to malign the gentleman. According to Richard Fitzwilliam, when he is in company with close friends, he can be quite witty and fun. Unfortunately, I have usually encountered him in public situations, where he is exceedingly reserved.'

'I know both to be true since I had the opportunity to observe him in public and private,' Elizabeth told her cousin.

'Now I am truly intrigued.' Alistair prompted, 'tell me all.'

After a minute's hesitation, Elizabeth gathered her courage and started to tell the tale of her encounters with the gentleman in Hertfordshire.

Alistair could not help but laugh when Lizzy mentioned that she had told Darcy 'Don't flatter yourself'.

'You must be the only woman who ever told him off. How did he take it?' Alistair was curious.

'Remarkably well,' replied Elizabeth. 'I must admit I have some sympathy for him being hunted by every fortune-hunter. I suppose you would know about those women. You are in a similar position, except that you have a title as well as everything else. Will you also be looking for a wife with a title, a large dowry and highly placed connections?'

'Also? I think I know where this story is going. You two like each other, but you are hiding your status, and he thinks he is duty-bound to marry someone with money and connections. Titled even. How close to the truth am I?' Alistair asked.

'Right on the mark,' admitted Lizzy. She then laid out the whole sorry tale for her cousin.

'I think I see what grandmother is planning,' speculated Alistair when Elizabeth had finished her story. 'If you are seen in my company when people do not know our family relationship, they would assume that I am interested in you. And if even a very eligible Duke is interested in this country nobody...'

'Then I should be more than good enough for a country gentleman, even if his uncle is an Earl,' Elizabeth finished for him. 'I expect you are correct.'

'In that case, I shall be most attentive to you. I have always wanted to see Darcy display some emotion. This could be fun,' he grinned mischievously. 'But seriously, you could marry just about anybody in the ton, why settle for Darcy?'

'Because he takes me seriously. When we have a discussion, he listens to me and my opinions. He treats me with respect. He is very considerate and protective of anyone he cares about.' Elizabeth could not resist to add, 'he is also very handsome, and he has the most devastating smile. He even has dimples when he smiles.'

'Dimples?'

'Dimples.'

~~DL~~

11 Games

1812

Alistair was indeed stunned when he met Jane again the following day. As a young girl, her looks had promised to be exceptional when she grew up. Now that promise had been fulfilled. Alistair was more than happy to be seen with the sisters on his arms.

After a relaxing dinner, the party adjourned to the theatre. Alistair was very pleased to enter the building with Elizabeth and Jane since he enjoyed the envious looks from many of the gentlemen. He assumed that the sour looks of the ladies were caused by the beauty of his cousins.

They had timed their arrival to perfection. It was only a few minutes till the start of the performance, which meant they could not stop and talk to anyone. Alistair just smiled and nodded at acquaintances while he led his group to his box. He seated the ladies at the front of the box while he and Gardiner took the seats in the rear.

Looking around the theatre, Alistair noticed Richard Fitzwilliam with his parents in a box on the other side of the theatre. He also recognised Darcy in the same box. Because of the family resemblance, the young girl with them, he assumed to be Miss Georgiana Darcy.

He leaned forward to whisper to Elizabeth and his Aunt. 'Grandmother's plan appears to be working even better than she had hoped. There is a certain Derbyshire gentleman in a box with the Earl of Matlock.'

'I hope he enjoys the show,' murmured Mrs Bennet with a mischievous smile at her double entendre.

The performance of Much Ado About Nothing was excellent, and all in their company became engrossed in it, unlike many other patrons who came to see and be seen. Many looks were directed at the Duke and his companions. Alistair was partially aware of this since this was familiar to him, but he ignored it to enjoy the play.

During the interval, he was unsurprised when the Fitzwilliam party entered their box.

The Countess of Matlock addressed Alistair, 'Your Grace, it is good to see you in company again. I was sorry to hear about your father but did not have the chance to tell you so in person.'

Alistair smiled charmingly, 'Lady Susan, you must be the only person who was sorry about my father's demise. But I thank you for your sentiments.'

Colonel Fitzwilliam chuckled at his words. 'You have not changed since Cambridge, still as honest as always.'

'It saves effort. Will you introduce me to your charming companion?'

'Since you already know my parents and Darcy could never be called charming, you must mean my ward and Darcy's sister, Miss Georgiana Darcy.' Turning to Georgie, he completed the introduction. 'Georgie this is His Grace, Alistair Flinter, the Duke of Denton.'

Georgiana blushed as she curtsied and murmured, 'A pleasure to meet you, Your Grace.'

'The pleasure is all mine.' Then he addressed the group, 'allow me to introduce my friends.'

He proceeded to introduce the whole company to each other.

Darcy was his usual tongue-tied self, but the Earl, Lady Susan and Colonel Fitzwilliam carried the conversation on their group's behalf, although the Colonel kept stealing glances at Jane. Jane managed a few quiet words with Georgiana to put her at ease.

'Are you perchance staying with the Dowager Duchess while you are in town?' Lady Susan asked Alistair. When he confirmed that he did, she added, 'it must be such a comfort to her to have family with her. It has been much too long since I had a chance to meet with the lady. I hope it is agreeable to her if I call on her?'

The Duke allowed that his grandmother would be pleased to see an old friend.

Lady Susan now turned to Mrs Bennet, 'I would be delighted to have you join me for tea when it is convenient. If you give me your direction, I will send you an invitation.' At Mrs Bennet's pointed look, Mr Gardiner complied.

It was nearly the end of the interval before Lady Susan and her company left the Denton box.

Alistair smirked at the others. 'Is everyone happy with the proceedings?'

'You were superb, my dear Alistair,' complimented Mrs Bennet. 'Mother could not have done better.'

'That is high praise indeed,' Alistair graciously accepted the compliment.

'And if looks could kill, you would now be dead. Mr Darcy is not at all pleased with you.'

The only response was an impertinent and unrepentant grin.

~~DL~~

Over the next few days, the Duke was busy with arranging the redecoration of Grover House.

When he was at Denton House, he noticed a suppressed air of excitement and amusement amongst the ladies. He decided that their scheming was too much for his delicate sensibilities and removed to his club for an evening of relaxation.

It turned out not to be as relaxing as he had hoped. He was approached by several of the other guests congratulating him on his exquisite mistress. Each time he denied the rumour. But more men kept mentioning Elizabeth.

Eventually, he decided to clarify the situation for all. He stood and called for everyone's attention.

'Gentlemen, it has come to my attention that there is a rather nasty rumour about me being bandied about. Let me make it quite clear. I do not now and never did have a mistress.'

He grinned at the shocked expressions of the other men. 'I am sorry to spoil your fun in spreading salacious gossip, but the ladies whom I escorted to the theatre the other night, are all dear friends of my grandmother, the Dowager Duchess. She does not take kindly to scurrilous rumours being spread about her friends. All of whom I have known most of my life.'

One of the men declared, 'according to what I was told, Miss Bingley knows both the young women and she claims that they are no better than they should be.'

Alistair smirked, 'can you tell me what the envious daughter of a tradesman could gain by maligning her betters?'

One of the men spoke up. 'Trying to eliminate her competition. But the way she is going about it is low, even for her.'

Alistair shrugged. 'What can I say...'

~~DL~~

The following afternoon brought a new source of amusement for the Duke when a group of visitors arrived.

The dowager had received a note from Mrs Gardiner, telling her that Elizabeth had been attacked by George Wickham, but was safe, only shaken, due to the timely arrival of Mr Darcy and Colonel Fitzwilliam.

A few minutes later, Elizabeth walked into the blue parlour on the arm of none other than Fitzwilliam Darcy. They were followed by Jane with Colonel Fitzwilliam and the Gardiners.

When Elizabeth was distracted by a bout of relieved weeping in Mrs Bennet's arms, Alistair took it upon himself to make the introductions to his grandmother, leaving out her relationship to Elizabeth.

Everyone settled into seats, and it was not long before Elizabeth regained her composure and settled in a chair near Darcy.

Edward Gardiner spoke up. 'Mr Darcy, earlier you asked me a question, which you wanted to address to Elizabeth's nearest male relative since her father is not in town. As much as I love Elizabeth as a niece, she is only my niece by courtesy. Her nearest male relation is sitting over there.' He indicated Alistair.

Darcy looked thunderstruck, glancing between Gardiner, Alistair, Elizabeth, and Mrs Bennet.

Alistair smirked. 'Did you have something to say to me, Darcy?'

Darcy swallowed convulsively. 'What is your relationship to Miss Elizabeth?'

'*Lady* Elizabeth is my cousin,' replied the duke, emphasising *Lady*.

'A distant cousin?' Darcy probed further.

'Not exactly. Since Mrs Bennet, or Lady Francine as is her proper title, is my aunt, sister to my late father.'

Darcy was speechless.

'Now that all this is cleared up, I gather you have something to ask me, Darcy?' The Duke asked again with a smug grin.

'That is something usually asked in private,' Darcy protested when he felt Elizabeth squeezing his hand.

She now addressed the Duke. 'Alistair you have had your fun. Now stop it. Mr Darcy has asked me to marry him, and I have accepted. You can add your stamp of approval or mind your own business. This day has been fraught enough. I really do not need you playing games.'

For the first time since their arrival, the Dowager made her presence known. 'Brava, Lizzy. I am proud of you,' she applauded. Then she addressed Darcy with a grin. 'Welcome to the family, my boy.'

Alistair was happy to second the sentiment.

~~DL~~

One afternoon when Alistair returned to Denton House from checking up on the progress of the redecoration of Grover House, he walked past the open door of the library.

He heard a familiar voice say teasingly, 'it was wise of you to show such a stern demeanour when in society.' Lizzy said impishly, 'you have a devastating smile. I fell in love with those dimples at that first assembly. If the other ladies had known you had dimples as well as wealth and position, you would never have survived society without being compromised.'

'Do you mean to tell me that you would choose a husband based on whether he had dimples? I had thought you much more discerning than that,' Darcy replied in the same tone of voice, surprising the Duke. Alistair had not thought that Darcy could have a playful side.

'It was what caught my eye. After that, when we had all those conversations, I loved how you listened to me. You never dismissed my opinions out of hand even when you disagreed with them. Do you have any idea how rare it is to have a serious conversation with a man?' Lizzy sounded almost wistful now.

'I will always listen to you. I may disagree with you, but I will always listen and consider your opinions. I promise you that,' said Darcy.

It became quiet after that, and Alistair debated whether to enter the library to ensure propriety but decided that with the door open they could not get up to too much mischief and a few kisses would not harm anyone.

~~DL~~

Alistair found the rest of the week rather amusing. The ladies had schemed to deal with Caroline Bingley for spreading the rumour about Elizabeth being his mistress.

When Miss Bingley, as expected, made a scene at the Worthington ball, declaring that 'Elizabeth Bennet is a penniless little nobody from the country who last year spent weeks trying to get her claws into Mr Darcy. He had more sense than to fall for her charms. Now she obviously has had more success with the duke.'

Alistair stood to his full height and looked down at Caroline.

'How dare you speak such lies, Madam. You will apologise to the lady immediately,' he demanded in ringing tones.

'Why should I for speaking the truth,' Caroline blustered. 'Do you know who this little chit is?'

'I know precisely who she is. Do you?'

Miss Bingley's world fell apart when she was informed that the lady, she had just insulted was Lady Elizabeth Fellmar, daughter of Earl James Fellmar and Lady Francine Fellmar and the granddaughter of the Dowager Duchess of Denton, which made Lady Elizabeth the Duke's cousin. In her eagerness to best a rival, she had committed the biggest faux pas anyone could have imagined. She would never be able to show her face in town again.

The situation deteriorated even further for her when Darcy declared that Elizabeth was his intended and that Caroline would not be welcome in any of his homes, she would not be allowed to use his name to gain entrance to polite society, and he would give her the cut direct if she ever crossed his path again.'

The final nail in the coffin of her ambition came when Bingley told her that he would see his solicitor to release her dowry and that he would set her up in her own establishment, effectively telling the world that she was on the shelf.

Although the Duke was very liberal in his views and attitudes, he also had a wide streak of the protective nobleman who safeguarded the women in his life. He was therefore pleased to have the vicious harpy put in her place.

~~DL~~

Two days later, a similar scene played out at Darcy House, when Lady Catherine barged in and insulted his cousin and his aunt.

Lady Catherine was very vocal when she objected to Darcy wanting to marry Elizabeth rather than her daughter Anne. Luckily for her, when she was throwing insults around, only family were present.

When she found out that one of the ladies she had insulted, was the daughter of the Dowager Duchess of Denton, Lady Catherine had fainted. The shock of being so badly mistaken about the identity of Elizabeth and having made such a fool of herself in front of the Dowager, who had caught her trying to compromise her son many years earlier, was too much for her.

Again, Alistair could not feel much pity toward the woman who had been determined to destroy his cousin's happiness.

~~DL~~

12 Overtures

1812

The Dowager and Alistair were having a quiet dinner together, the Bennet family having returned to Meryton the previous day. 'How is your redecorating coming along?' she enquired of her grandson.

'The painting and papering are finished. The new drapes will be hung next week. I have also discovered several good paintings in the attic. They are being cleaned now and should be ready any day. As you know, I have made some changes to the staff. I now have maids who are competent rather than purely decorative. The only thing I am still missing is a hostess. But aside from that, if all goes well, I will be able to move by the end of next week. You will get your peace back, then.' He smiled at her. 'Not that I am not grateful that you allowed me to be your guest.'

The Dowager looked thoughtful and a little sad. She quietly asked, 'do you have to leave? Anne Hopkins is a wonderful companion and looks after me very well, but I have rather enjoyed having you around. Even if you are still the rascal that you have ever been.' At the last, her cheeky grin made a brief appearance. 'Also, it would be appropriate if the Duke of Denton stayed at Denton House while in town. In that case, you would not even have to look for a hostess. I would be exceedingly pleased to host dinner parties again.'

Alistair looked thoughtful. 'I admit, I would prefer to live here than at Grover House. Like you, I like to have family about and, apart from Robert, you have been my mainstay in the family for all of my life.' His demeanour lightened again. 'I would be happy to stay here while I am in town. In addition, since this has been your home for all these years, I will not insist on moving into the Master's suite, even though I am technically the head of the house.' He gave his grandmother his best mischievous smile. 'This new suite Barton put me into is rather nice, and I am happy to stay there.'

His grandmother laughed. 'I am overjoyed to hear that you like the Master's suite.' Now it was her turn to smile at his surprised look.

'You had Barton put me in the Master's suite?' he questioned. 'But I distinctly remember that Barton said it was the blue suite.'

'Yes, to both, my dear boy.' The Dowager started to explain. 'After Alexander died and you inherited the title, I thought it appropriate to make the Master's suite ready for you. I have been using the Mistress' suite ever since I married your grandfather. At the time I had it decorated to suit my taste, and after he died, I saw no reason to move. We may have to re-think the arrangement if you ever get married.'

Alistair sat there shaking his head. 'And here I thought you put me in a spare family suite because you had Aunt Francine and Elizabeth staying and had given one of them the room I used to occupy. But as for getting married, I do not think that will happen any time soon. I cannot bear those fawning, simpering flowers of society. Or the cold, calculating ones either.'

The Dowager responded, 'is that why you have not married? I had the impression that you did that to spite your father.'

'That it incensed my father was an advantage due to the argument he and I had for years. He kept insisting that I should marry someone suitable. It did not matter who or if I even liked her, as long as I produced an heir. Even better if I produced a spare as well.' He sounded disgusted. 'I cannot understand how a man who ignored me and my brother all my life had the audacity to tell me how to lead my life.'

'I presume he never mentioned why he did not wish for your company while you were growing up?' his grandmother asked.

'No, he did not. I always assumed, that since our mater was the daughter of the Duke of Cardic, his was an arranged marriage and once he had done his dynastic duty, he went back to his debauched ways.' Alistair shrugged.

'Oh dear, we have all been remiss in not explaining the situation properly,' sighed the Dowager.

'What was there to explain, his conduct was rather obvious.' Alistair was still dismissive.

'Your father's marriage to Lady Penelope was a true love match.' At Alistair's startled look, she nodded and continued. 'Unfortunately giving birth to twins was too much for your mother. Alexander was devastated and initially blamed you and your brother for his wife's death. Although we managed to convince him that you were not to blame, it pained him too much to see you and be constantly reminded of his lost love. You do look a lot like your mother. After that, he was determined never to feel such pain again.'

The Dowager sighed. 'Even though I cannot approve of his motives, I can understand them.'

Alistair shook his head. 'Although I can see his reasons, it changes nothing. He is still a stranger to me. Since he never allowed us to know him, I cannot feel sympathy for him. But why did you not tell me of this before? I remember you telling us that he was busy with affairs, which I used to think of as business affairs. Very careful choice of words, was it not?'

'I am so dreadfully sorry, Alistair. But I could not bring myself to tell you that your father resented your very existence. After you grew up, I had hoped that you and Robert would have that discussion with your father. That he would explain...'

'No, he never explained. He knew that Robert and I hated him. But he never made excuses.' He considered for a moment. 'I suppose I can at least respect him for that.' Alistair was thoughtful for a minute or two. 'Yes, that knowledge eases my memory of him. Thank you, grandmother.'

'I am happy that you feel better. But we were discussing your ideas about marriage.'

He gave her his brilliant smile. 'When I find a woman who is interested in me, rather than my title and I like her in return, I will consider marriage. Like Lizzy, I need a partner whom I can respect. Why do not you try to find me such a paragon?'

'Very well, I shall accept the challenge. But it will have to wait until after Elizabeth's wedding. I am for Netherfield next week to ensure the house is in order for all the guests.' The Dowager grinned. 'In the meantime, welcome to your home.'

~~DL~~

The following afternoon a letter arrived from the steward at Denton Manor. After reading the missive, the Duke immediately went to see the Dowager.

After greeting his grandmother briefly, he explained, 'I just received an express from Mr Carter. It appears there is some flooding at Denton Manor, and he needs my assistance. I will need to leave in the morning.'

'Is it the area near the Meadows estate? That has always been a problem since they cannot afford to put in proper drainage,' the Dowager queried.

'Yes, grandmother, you are correct as usual. This is the third time in the last ten years that the area is flooded. If Harper cannot afford to put in the drainage, I shall. I will not respect his pride any longer if it causes damage to my land and tenants.'

'Good. I was hoping you would be concerned for your tenants.' The Dowager smiled fondly at the Duke. 'I believe you are becoming a better master than even your grandfather was.'

'That is high praise indeed. But now I had better prepare for an early start tomorrow. I will see you at dinner?' At her nod, he left to find his valet.

~~DL~~

The Duke arrived at Denton Manor in the late afternoon. Mr Carter was waiting for him, having received the express the Duke had sent the day before. After only the briefest of greetings, he demanded. 'What news have you of the situation?'

'The eastern fields are under water. We have managed to relocate the livestock to the home farm. The Smith's cottage is knee-deep in water. I have taken the liberty to house them here for the moment. Mr Harper is adamant that he will take care of his own problems in his own time.'

'That time has come and gone. It needs to be fixed now. Give me a few minutes to get changed, then we will go to see the man.' After a day spent on the road, Alistair was in no mood to pander to his neighbour's pride any longer.

Mr Carter took the opportunity to have fresh horses harnessed to the Duke's carriage. By the time they were ready, so was Denton. On the drive to the Meadows, Carter provided more details of happenings at Denton Manor. The Duke was able to see some of the flooding as they passed the affected area.

Half an hour later they arrived at the neighbour's estate. Mr Harper was not thrilled to see the Duke. He knew he could fob off the steward, but the Duke was another matter.

'Good afternoon, Your Grace. It is good to see you. What gives me the pleasure of your visit?' Harper tried to appear nonchalant.

'Good afternoon, Mr Harper. I would have thought the reason is obvious. There is this small matter of a flood. Both on your fields and mine. Now, if it were only your fields that were flooded, I would not concern myself. Because then it would simply be your business, and I would not Interfere. But the drainage issue you have is impacting my land and my tenants. Therefore, I have come to discuss what we are going to do about the situation.'

'There is nothing to discuss, Your Grace. This is my land, and I can do what I choose,' Harper blustered.

Denton took a deep breath to calm himself. 'This drainage issue is impacting my land as well. I have therefore a vested interest. Because of that, I am prepared to share in the cost of the solution,' he offered.

Mr Harper was offended. 'I will have none of that. I will not accept charity. This is my land, and I will look after it as I see fit.'

Alistair finally lost his patience. He thundered, 'you obviously cannot look after your own estate, or mine would not be flooded for the third time. I tried to be civil about this, but you sir, are a stubborn fool. Your pride is what is keeping you poor. Yours could be a good estate if only you fixed the drainage problem. But you are caught in a vicious circle. You do not have the money to fix the drainage, and your waterlogged fields prevent you from earning the money to fix the drainage.'

'Not quite so proud as you think,' retorted Harper, but then some of the fight had gone out of him. 'I tried to borrow money from the bank. But since my harvests have been bad due to the wet fields, I cannot get a loan.' It was hard for him to admit to failure. His shoulders slumped when he said, 'you are correct, naming it a vicious circle. Very well, what do you suggest?'

Denton gave a sigh of relief. 'I propose that I will initially pay for the drainage to be fixed. Then you will repay two-thirds of the cost, using fifty percent of the extra profit you will make, until the cost is repaid.'

'So, you will wear one-third of the cost?' questioned Harper.

'Getting the drainage fixed will benefit my estate as well. It is well worth the expense to me.'

Now that they had reached this accord, the Duke, Mr Harper, and Mr Carter, who had quietly stayed in the background during the initial discussion, sat down to work out a plan of action.

When the details had been agreed upon, the Duke and his steward made their way back to Denton Manor. It was getting rather late, and they were tired, but on the whole, well satisfied with the outcome of the day.

Mrs Carter had a good supper ready for them, which they both enjoyed when they returned. After that, Alistair was very happy to see his bed. It had been an exceedingly long day.

~~DL~~

Alistair spent another three weeks at Denton Manor, ensuring that the plans they had made were carried out. By the end of that time, much of the drainage was in place, the fields were dry, and the Smiths and the livestock were back where they belonged.

Once the repairs to the water damage was complete, the Duke also insisted on replacing most of the goods that were destroyed by the water in his tenant's cottage. The Smiths were very grateful and lauded him as the best master they could have.

Alistair felt that the relatively small sum he had spent, was well worth it for the loyalty he had gained. He had learnt early on that tenants, who were well looked after, were healthier and therefore more productive. Which, in return, meant better profits in the long term and loyal tenants, who worked his lands for generations.

~~DL~~

13 Apologies

When his business at Denton Manor was taken care of, Denton returned to London to inspect the results of the refurbishment of Grover House.

He was well satisfied with the look of the decoration. The house now looked elegant, rich, but not ostentatious. After the inspection, Alistair went to see his man of business to arrange to let the property.

Once that was taken care of, he allowed himself a few days to relax, before travelling to Netherfield Park for his cousin's wedding the following week.

~~DL~~

Alistair woke slowly and savoured the leisure he could enjoy again. He was in no particular rush this day. He considered that leaving sometime around noon would give him sufficient time to get to Netherfield Park in the late afternoon without pushing the horses.

Eventually, his stomach told him it was time to get up. He rang for his valet to help him get ready for the day. Since he would be travelling, he opted for clothing designed more for comfort than the latest fashion.

He was just finishing a leisurely breakfast when a surprise visitor was announced.

He had a last mouthful of coffee, then rose to meet his visitor in the foyer.

'Lady Catherine, what an unexpected pleasure,' he greeted the lady cautiously.

The lady, whom he addressed, nodded calmly and announced, 'Your Grace, it is good of you to see me, but I begged an audience with the Dowager Duchess.'

Alistair was rather surprised at the way she phrased her request but assumed the lady was no longer the irate harridan he had met two months prior.

Giving her the benefit of doubt, he replied civilly, 'Lady Catherine I am afraid you made the visit for nought. My grandmother is not in town.'

Lady Catherine looked rather embarrassed. 'Since I pride myself on my frankness, please do me the courtesy and be frank with me, Your Grace. Is the Dowager Duchess out of town as you say, or is she simply not home to me? I can understand that she would not wish to see me after my behaviour at our last meeting.'

Alistair smiled at this statement. 'My grandmother is currently in Hertfordshire to see my cousin Elizabeth married. To your nephew.'

'I had not realised the wedding is so soon to happen. I have obviously not been invited. My family is rather put out with me.' Lady Catherine straightened her shoulders as if to face a firing squad. 'Your Grace, please, convey to your family my sincerest apologies for my deplorable behaviour back in February. I have had weeks to consider my behaviour and attitudes and with the help of my daughter and my rector have sought to improve both. I was convinced of my infallibility and was proven wrong. That was a bitter pill to swallow, but I believe it will benefit me in the long run.'

The Duke made a quick decision. 'Do you wish to make your apologies to my family in person?' he asked.

'I would like to do so very much, but since they are not available...'

'I am to leave for Netherfield within the hour. Would you like to accompany me?'

'I could not possibly intrude on your family at such a time,' Lady Catherine protested. 'In addition, both my daughter and my rector await me in the carriage.'

She now smiled somewhat ruefully. 'I suspect it is not so much to support me; which is their stated purpose; but to ensure I do not renege on my penance. At least they had the decency to await me in the carriage, rather than insist on witnessing my humiliation.'

'If your wish for reconciliation is sincere, I expect my current and future families would be happy for you to attend the wedding,' Alistair suggested.

'Even if they do not wish for my company at that joyous event, now that I have come this far, I would like to make what amends I may,' replied Lady Catherine.

~~DL~~

Two carriages pulled up in front of Netherfield. The first contained only Alistair and his valet; Lady Catherine having declined his invitation to travel with him.

Their approach had been noted, and since Alistair was expected, the Dowager, Mrs Bennet and Elizabeth stepped outside to greet their relative.

Alistair alighted from the first carriage without bothering to wait for a footman to place the steps for him.

He hurried to the ladies to greet them. 'Good afternoon, Grandmother, Aunt, Cousin. Brace yourselves, you are about to get an apology from Lady Catherine. At least that is her stated purpose for the visit.'

The Dowager raised an eyebrow and murmured, 'indeed,' before turning to greet the visitor.

Lady Catherine exited her carriage with more decorum, having waited for a footman to place the step and hand her out.

'Good afternoon, Your Grace. Good afternoon, Lady Francine, Lady Elizabeth. I am pleased that you are all here.' Lady Catherine nodded politely at the ladies and took a deep breath before continuing.

'I have come to tender my deepest apologies to you both for my abominable behaviour at our last meeting. There was no excuse for such vitriolic abuse and slander, which I spouted that day. It has taken some time for me to realise that my arrogance and belief in my own infallibility were completely misplaced. As was my determination to control the life of my nephew. It has been brought home to me that I am as fallible as all the people I have previously despised.'

It was obvious to her audience how much the effort cost the proud woman. 'Thank you for doing me the courtesy of listening to me. I will not trouble you any longer. Good day.' Lady Catherine again nodded politely and turned to leave.

The Dowager was concerned about the sincerity of the apology but considering the effort it must have taken to deliver such a humbling speech, decided to give Lady Catherine the benefit of doubt.

'I accept your apology, Lady Catherine,' she announced. After a brief look at her daughter and granddaughter, who both nodded agreement, she offered. 'If you would care to see your nephew being married, you are welcome to stay.'

'I thank you, but I would not wish to impose on your family at this time,' Lady Catherine said hesitantly.

Mrs Bennet seconded her mother's offer. 'Lady Catherine, in two days you will be our family too. I would like to see us as one family.'

Lady Catherine's countenance showed her chagrin at the generosity of the ladies she had previously insulted. 'If you are certain that I will not intrude...'

'Nonsense. As my daughter said, you will be our family, and you already are family to both grooms. I insist that you stay unless you have no wish to do so,' said the Dowager

'Both grooms? Who else is getting married?' Came the startled exclamation from Anne de Bourgh who had exited the carriage and had been waiting quietly in the background with William Collins.

'I am sorry, were you not aware that Richard Fitzwilliam is marrying Jane?'

'Cousin Richard is also getting married? That is wonderful news,' cried Anne.

'If Richard is your cousin, you must be Miss Anne de Bourgh,' said Mrs Bennet with a smile.

'My apologies for my lapse in manners,' said Lady Catherine. 'Your Grace, Lady Francine, Lady Elizabeth, please allow me to introduce to you my daughter Anne de Bourgh. Anne, it is my honour to introduce to you the Dowager Duchess of Denton, her daughter Lady Francine Bennet and her granddaughter Lady Elizabeth.'

Anne curtsied and replied, 'it is an honour to meet you.'

'I am pleased to make your acquaintance,' replied the Dowager with a smile. 'I have heard a great deal about you from your cousins.'

'Please disregard whatever you heard about me from Richard. He notoriously embellishes his stories,' said Anne with an embarrassed smile.

'That is a foul calumny,' the man just mentioned said from behind her. 'All my stories are the absolute truth. At least from my perspective.' Richard grinned.

'Richard, I just heard that congratulations are in order,' Anne smiled at her cousin and the stunning young woman who was gently holding his arm.

'They are indeed, and I would thank you to keep all the things you know about me to yourself. At least until after the wedding. I would not wish you to frighten her off,' teased Richard before making the introductions.

'What is the occasion for your visit?' Richard enquired of Anne, but his aunt answered.

'I had to make some apologies. I may be a fool, but I am not stupid. I know when I am wrong. It simply takes me a long time to admit it.'

While Richard greeted his aunt and cousin and performed the introduction to his intended, William Collins approached Mrs Bennet. 'May I add my most humble apologies, Lady Francine. I was unaware of Cousin Bennet's bereavement and second marriage to such an illustrious lady as yourself. I would never have presumed that I was worthy of any of your daughters had I but known of your antecedents,' said Collins with remarkable brevity.

'I accept your apology, Cousin Collins. Now, since it appears that you are all staying, shall we move inside where it is more comfortable, and you can refresh yourselves.'

~~DL~~

Mrs Nicholls, efficient as ever, had suspected that more people would need to be accommodated, sent her staff to prepare rooms for the visitors. When the party entered, she approached the Dowager and said quietly, 'I have had three rooms prepared in the guest-wing.'

'Excellent, you are as efficient and perceptive as always.'

The Dowager turned to her unexpected guests. 'Mrs Nicholls will show you to your rooms so that you may refresh yourselves. Tea will be served in the drawing-room in half an hour.

~~DL~~

14 Wedding

Since Alistair was ready early, he decided to collect a book to while away the time before dinner. When he approached, the door to the library was partially open.

As he pushed the door open completely and stepped inside, he was confronted by an unexpected sight.

His cousin Elizabeth and Darcy were in a heated embrace and sharing a passionate kiss, which was just coming to an end.

Elizabeth slowly pulled her lips away from Darcy, only to lean her head against his shoulder as she murmured, 'I am looking forward to tomorrow when we do not have to stop.'

Darcy, whose eyes were still closed while his breathing slowed down, responded with a contented, 'Hmmm,' while tightening his arms around her body.

'I am thankful I know that you two are getting married tomorrow. Otherwise, I would be most shocked by your behaviour, Cousin,' Alistair said with mock severity.

Darcy's eyes flew open as he pulled himself up to his full height, but he drew Elizabeth even closer in an unconscious protective gesture.

'Oh fiddlesticks, do not try to tell me you have never kissed a girl, cousin,' Elizabeth replied dismissively as she lifted her head from Darcy's shoulder to look at Alistair challengingly.

'Not like that. I certainly have never kissed a girl like that.' Alistair was almost wistful with his response.

'In that case, why do you not go and find yourself a girl to kiss like that and leave us in peace,' was the completely unexpected response from Darcy, who looked at Alistair with a mischievous grin, which was reminiscent of his cousin Richard.

'It appears you are not just the stuffed shirt and wet blanket I always thought you to be. There is hope for you yet,' laughed Alistair as he stepped back out of the room. 'I shall leave you to your amusements. But do not take too long. Dinner is not far off.'

~~DL~~

The last dinner before the weddings was a very pleasant affair. The two families appeared to get on very well.

As the hostess, the Dowager presided over the company at the head of the table, while Elizabeth, as the owner of the estate, sat at the foot of the table. The Earl was at the Dowager's right, and Darcy was seated to the right of Elizabeth. The rest of the families was spread out in between.

Looking around Alistair realised that of the five and twenty people seated around the dining table, there were only two who were not family. Charles Bingley, who had arrived this afternoon to stand with Darcy at the wedding and Charlotte Lucas, who had been invited by Elizabeth and was placed at Alistair's left.

'Miss Lucas, will you be standing with my cousin tomorrow?' asked Alistair.

'No, Your Grace, Eliza and Jane have enough sisters to stand with them. Any more attendants would have been too much of a spectacle. But she is my oldest friend, and I think she wanted me to not feel left out.' Charlotte smiled serenely.

'I gather you have known her for a long time then?'

'Most of her life. Even though she is much younger than I am, I was drawn to her lively personality. I suppose the education she received from both her parents made her a little more mature than most girls her age at the time,' Charlotte was happy to reminisce.

Alistair laughed. 'I remember when I first met my cousin. She was sitting in a tree, and I mistook her for a servant's daughter. I behaved rather badly, and she took me to task for it. My brother has never let me forget that, at the very mature age of four and ten, I was bested by a six-year-old girl.'

'I can imagine her doing that since I met her at about the same time, although I was only two and ten.' Charlotte smiled fondly. 'Come to think of it, when I first saw her, she was also sitting in a tree. I was concerned that she might have climbed the tree to hide from something, but when I asked her what she was doing in the tree, she told me she was keeping an eye on the baby birds.'

'That does sound like my cousin. Elizabeth has always been curious and protective,' Alistair agreed. 'From what I have seen, she and Darcy are well suited. I hope they will be very happy together.'

They continued to discuss Elizabeth. In the process, Alistair learnt much about Miss Lucas since it was impossible for her to narrate the stories without including some of her own history and opinions.

Charlotte, in turn, found that she quite approved of Eliza's cousin. He might be a Duke, but he was not snobbish now and surprisingly good company.

Before they knew it, dinner was finished, and the ladies withdrew to the drawing-room to give the gentlemen a brief chance to toast the grooms amongst themselves.

~~DL~~

Alistair thought it amusing that Bingley, who normally had the easy manners to be happy in any company, was the one person in the group to be self-conscious. Whereas Darcy was relaxed and smiling.

'What is the matter, Bingley? I have never known you to be ill at ease in company. Darcy yes, but never you,' Alistair asked the young man.

'To be honest, I feel rather like an intruder. I am the only outsider in this group. Yes, I have been invited to dinner parties with Darcy and his peers, but this is the first time I have attended a *family* dinner with such elevated company.' Bingley looked somewhat embarrassed when he explained this.

'I know my family, and from what I know of Richard and his family, they all have one thing in common,' Alistair started to soothe the young man when he was interrupted.

'Unlike me, they are all of the first circles,' interjected Bingley somewhat morosely.

'Not completely true, but what I was trying to tell you is that they are more concerned with character than position. What they care about is that you are an honourable man. You have been Darcy's friend for, what is it now, a decade? In that time, you have never tried to use him to your advantage.'

'He has opened doors for me, which I could never have aspired to on my own merits.'

'It was your own merits which made him invite you. And you helped him navigate social situations in which he is woefully inept.' Alistair grinned. 'Cheer up. If you were not his friend, he would not have asked you to stand with him tomorrow.'

Bingley looked a little more cheerful at this pronouncement. 'You may have the right of it at that.'

~~DL~~

When they re-joined the ladies, Alistair sought out Miss Lucas to continue their conversation. He found her company to be both exciting and soothing.

Once she had gotten over the fact that Elizabeth's cousin was a Duke, but quite human, she had relaxed and conversed with him in an unaffected manner.

Alistair thoroughly enjoyed their conversation, to the point where his grandmother and Elizabeth were exchanging meaningful glances, which he did not even notice.

At last, but much too soon for Alistair, the evening came to an end.

Elizabeth declared, 'I must seek my bed. It would not do for a bride to be late for her wedding.'

This announcement broke up the gathering. The party from Longbourne and Miss Lucas said their farewells and left in the Bennet carriage.

Alistair stared after it while it was visible. He had come to Netherfield only for the wedding. He was due to leave the day after. Now he reconsidered his departure date.

There was something about Miss Lucas. While not conventionally pretty, she had a presence he found exceedingly attractive and intriguing. Unlike Lady Francesca, who was stunningly beautiful on the surface but had no depth, Miss Lucas made him feel like he could tell her anything.

He needed time to find out more.

He approached the Dowager. 'Grandmother, would it inconvenience you if I stayed a little longer than planned?' he asked.

'Not at all, my dear boy. I would welcome your company. It has been a long time since we have had a chance to come together as a family. I am certain that Francine, Thomas, and the girls would also enjoy having you around for as long as you want to stay. In a few weeks, Jane and Richard will settle into Longbourn. At about that time Elizabeth and Darcy will spend a few days here to collect Georgiana, before going to London for some shopping. If only Robert could be here, the family would be complete.'

~~DL~~

The wedding ceremony, although joyful for all concerned, was unremarkable. Everyone responded appropriately at the correct time, and in short order, the formality was concluded when Mr and Mrs Darcy, as well as Mr and Mrs Fitzwilliam, signed the register.

The wedding party adjourned to Longbourn for the Wedding Breakfast. The brides and grooms were toasted, delicious food was consumed, and speeches were given and applauded.

As soon as they could do so, Mr and Mrs Darcy said their goodbyes and left for London and Darcy House, where they would spend a few days before setting off on a wedding tour.

Mr and Mrs Fitzwilliam had been offered the use of Denton House, while the Dowager and Alistair stayed at Netherfield with the Bennets.

~~DL~~

15 Again?

The wedding was over, and the remaining guests were planning to leave Netherfield the following morning. Everyone had decided on an early evening to allow for an early start the next day.

Lady Catherine entered her daughter's bedroom. Anne had already changed to go to bed. Her mother looked her up and down as if she were a side of beef hanging in a butcher's window.

'Your dress is adequate, but we have to do something about your hair,' she announced. Suiting words to actions, she stepped up to her daughter and pulled the pins and ribbons out of her hair. She then proceeded to make it artfully dishevelled.

At first, Anne was too stunned to object. When she, at last, found her voice, she protested. 'Mother, what are you doing? You are messing up my hair!'

'Hush, girl. You need to look convincing. Otherwise, no one will believe you have just been ravished by the Duke.' Lady Catherine explained impatiently.

'I do not wish to be ravished by the Duke or anyone else,' Anne baulked at the idea.

'You do not need to *be* ravished, as long as everyone believes you were. Then the Duke will have to do the honourable thing and marry you.' Her mother was getting rather exasperated with Anne's objections.

'There is nothing honourable about trapping somebody into a marriage they do not want. I will not do it.' Anne pleaded, 'please, mother, give up this appalling scheme. I want nothing to do with it.'

Lady Catherine hissed. 'You will do as you are told, my girl. You will marry the Duke and combine the great estates of Rosings and Denton. Now enough of your hysterics. You will come with me.' With that, Lady

Catherine took Anne's arm in a surprisingly firm grip and started to pull her from the room.

'Mother, please, stop it.' Anne struggled to break free of her mother's grip, but it was too strong.

Lady Catherine dragged Anne all the way to the family wing, where she knew the Duke's rooms were. Since Anne did not want to be made a spectacle of, she did not dare to raise her voice.

'Mother, I will not marry him even if you strip me stark naked and throw me into his arms.' Anne tried one final time to make her mother see reason.

'For once you have a good idea,' gloated her mother, as she grabbed hold of the edge of Anne's robe and jerked. The robe and nightgown ripped. 'Perfect. Now you will go in there and do your duty to me.' the Lady hissed.

'Really Catherine, first you try to compromise my son. Now you try to make your daughter compromise my grandson. Will you never learn?' The Dowager's silky tones cut through Lady Catherine like a dagger. She whirled around and was confronted not only by the Dowager, who was standing in the open doorway of the room across the hall but also her brother and his wife, both looking grim.

The door to the Duke's room opened, revealing Mrs Bennet. 'Anne, how good of you to join us. But you must be a touch chilly. Here, have my shawl.' With that, Mrs Bennet covered Anne's torn robe with her shawl and put her arm around her comfortingly. She gently pulled her into the room.

'You again!' Lady Catherine screamed at the Dowager. 'Why do you always have to foil my plans! I went to so much trouble making everyone believe that I had become the simpering little nobody you wanted me to be! I even apologised to you and your daughter! Do you have any idea how much I wanted to cast up my accounts when I did that? But I did it so that I could get Anne into a position to catch the Duke. And all of it is for nothing!!!' She rushed at the Dowager with her hands stretched out, and her fingers curled like claws.

Her brother stepped in front of the Dowager. He grabbed his sister's arms and shook her. 'Stop it, Cathy. Get a grip on yourself. This will do you no good.'

His sister did not appear to hear him. 'Let me go. I want to kill her. Let go of me!' She struggled to free herself.

The commotion had attracted the attention of two footmen, who at a nod from the Earl of Matlock took hold of Lady Catherine.

'My sister has become overwrought. She needs something to calm her down. Please take her to her room and ensure she stays there. I will have something sent for her.'

~~DL~~

When the footmen had dragged the raving woman away, Andrew Fitzwilliam turned to the Dowager, who had stepped back into the sitting room of the suite where she had gathered the witnesses. 'I am sorry, Amelia, that you were inconvenienced like this. But how did you know?' Now that they were family, they had agreed to forego formal address while amongst family.

'That was my doing, Sir,' announced Collins who had been sitting quietly out of view of the door. 'Lady Catherine takes me for granted and sometimes forgets that I am in the room. This afternoon I heard her muttering to herself about making Miss de Bourgh catch His Grace tonight. I happen to know that Miss de Bourgh has no interest in the Duke, and I did not wish for her to be forced into a life she did not care for. I am afraid I betrayed Lady Catherine's confidence and approached cousin Bennet for his advice.'

'Thomas came to me,' the Dowager continued the explanation. 'I thought it best to let your sister carry out her plan and step in at the appropriate time. I wanted you here as the head of her family, to take whatever measures might be necessary. I had not realised how bad things had become. I considered her excessively ambitious but sane. But that exhibition tonight makes me think she needs medical attention. I am sorry, Andrew.'

'I am afraid you are right. I will take her to London tomorrow and find a doctor. We may have to find a way to confine her. With our support, Anne can take over her inheritance a little early.' Fitzwilliam sighed. 'But why did you not say anything about this to me?'

'Because we were not certain she would go through with her plan. We were not even certain that was a plan, rather than just hyperbole. But if she was determined to force the issue, I wanted there to be no doubt and I wanted her stopped. Permanently. But because you are family, I was hoping for it to be done quietly.' Amelia smiled sadly.

'Cathy was never quiet. But I had better go and see to her.' He offered his arm to his wife. 'Will you come with me, my dear?'

~~DL~~

As the couple left, the Dowager went across the hall and knocked on the door. Her daughter opened the door and invited her in.

Anne de Bourgh sat on a sofa in the sitting room with a cup of tea and a glass of brandy. She looked like she had been crying but appeared to be recovering.

'Anne, how are you feeling?' the Dowager asked.

'Better thank you. How is my mother?'

'Your uncle is taking her to London in the morning for medical attention.'

Anne nodded. 'I understand. I was afraid that she was not herself lately but had not realised how bad she had become. She has been obsessed with marrying me off to Cousin Darcy. I think his marriage to Elizabeth may have been what pushed her into insanity.'

Lady Francine patted Anne's hand. 'I am certain your uncle will do what is best for her. Since it is safe to leave this room, shall I take you to yours?'

'Thank you, that would be exceedingly kind of you. I feel suddenly very tired.' Anne stood up. 'Thank you, Lady Amelia.'

'Good night, mother,' Lady Francine said as she escorted Anne out of the room.

The Dowager raised her voice. 'It is safe to come out now.'

The door to the bedroom opened. Alistair stepped into the room saying, 'thank heavens this is over. That was rather embarrassing. Poor Anne, having a mother like that.'

'Yes, but everything is taken care of for now. I am for bed. I will see you in the morning. Good night, Alistair,' the Dowager said tiredly.

'Good night, grandmother.'

~~DL~~

When she returned to her rooms, the Dowager reflected on the discussion after the visitor's arrival on Monday afternoon.

She had sent Lady Catherine and her party off with Mrs Nicholls. 'Alistair, a word, if you please,' she stopped her grandson from following Mrs Nicholls. 'You too,' she indicated to the others.

The Dowager led the way into the drawing-room where Darcy was waiting for the ladies' return.

'Did I hear the dulcet tones of Aunt Catherine just now?' he queried.

'You did indeed. She came to tender her apologies for her behaviour at your house. We invited her, her daughter and Mr Collins to stay,' replied the Dowager.

'What do you make of this situation?' she asked when everyone had settled into seats.

'She seemed genuine enough,' declared Alistair. 'Richard, you know her better than we do, what are your thoughts?'

'It has cost her a great deal to come here and apologise,' Richard said thoughtfully. 'I cannot remember ever hearing her apologise. Her pride must hurt abominably. For her to do so, she must have an excellent reason, and I simply cannot believe she has had that great a change of heart. She may wish to be in your good books since she will now need to look for a husband for Anne.'

Now his usual grin appeared again. 'Although I suspect Anne will look for herself without regard for her mother. Anne will be five and twenty next month and come into her inheritance. Anne is the heir of Rosings. At which point, Aunt Catherine loses her power over the estate.'

'It just occurs to me that you, Alistair, and Darcy had better lock your bedroom doors while my aunt is in residence. She might try to throw Anne into either one of your beds. She has coveted Pemberley for years, but Denton Manor would be an even bigger plum. It would also remove Anne from Rosings, leaving her in charge.'

'So, you are suggesting that we should be wary,' mused Mrs Bennet.

Alistair smiled at Lady Francine. 'Aunt, do you remember those battles you helped us recreate when we were boys? Beware of Greeks bearing gifts. And keep in mind that Richard was a Colonel in his Majesty's army. Strategy is second nature to him.'

'You counsel caution then,' nodded the Dowager. 'What about you, Richard. Will you also lock your bedroom door?'

'I will, although there is no need to do so. Aunt Catherine very definitely does not want me as Master of Rosings.' Richard smiled cynically.

'Very well. We will all be civil, in case the apology was genuine, but we will also exercise caution.'

~~DL~~

The following morning, the Earl of Matlock again apologised for his sister's behaviour. 'I will be taking her to London with me immediately after breakfast. In town, I will consult a doctor who specialises in obsessions, to see if he can help Cathy.'

He smiled sadly. 'She seems to have had a brainstorm. Hopefully, he or someone he knows can help her. But whatever happens, I will ensure that she cannot embarrass the family again.'

'Anne and Mr Collins will follow us to London, where we will arrange to have Anne confirmed as the Mistress of Rosings. I hope we will meet again soon under better circumstances.'

~~DL~~

Before Anne left, she requested an interview with the Dowager and the Duke.

'I am grateful for your intervention last night. But you should know that I was not going to marry Lord Denton, no matter what happened. Since my mother flaunts propriety, I saw no reason to be bound by it either. If I was compromised by her actions, I was quite prepared to remain unmarried, rather than be miserable in a forced marriage.'

Now a sly smile spread over Anne's face. 'My inheritance is not bound to my being married. With the law and Uncle Andrew on my side, mother would have been most unhappy living in the Dower House in circumstances she can afford since I am not prepared to support her profligate lifestyle.'

~~DL~~

William Collins was the final person to take his leave.

'I am sorry that my initial ignorance caused this chain of events. You have been most gracious to forgive my blundering.'

'Cousin Collins, you have more than made up for any failings by your timely warning. We truly appreciate your assistance in preventing a travesty.'

'It was the right thing to do. You are family, and Lady Catherine was acting dishonourably. I could not permit her to succeed. I only hope that Miss de Bourgh can forgive my transgression against her mother.'

Alistair smiled, 'I am certain you will find that Miss de Bourgh is also grateful for your assistance.'

'I hope so. I think she is a remarkable lady,' Collins said with a wistful look.

Alistair offered his hand to Collins. 'Good luck, Cousin Collins.'

Collins was struck speechless by this address. He simply took the proffered hand and bowed respectfully before leaving.

~~DL~~

16 Getting acquainted

Over the next few days, the Bennet family was busy moving into Netherfield. Although the servants were doing the actual work, everyone had to make last-minute decisions about what to take with them and what to leave behind. When Jane and Richard moved into Longbourn, they would be able to make any changes that they wished.

'Grandmother, would you do something for me?' Alistair asked the Dowager one morning after the family had settled in.

'What can I do, that a young and fit man cannot do for himself?' she replied with a grin.

'You could ask Miss Lucas to tea,' Alistair suggested. 'Whereas it would be most improper if I were to invite her.'

'Miss Lucas?' his grandmother was intrigued. She had noticed his interest during the dinner before the wedding but was still surprised by the request. 'Of course, I would be delighted to invite her.' Now she grinned. 'I can even be hard of hearing if you wish.'

'No thank you. I would like a chance to learn more about her. You might be able to draw her out more than would be proper for me.'

'You mean a nosey old woman can ask questions which a handsome young man cannot.'

'I would not have put it that way, but yes thank you.'

~~DL~~

Charlotte Lucas became a frequent visitor at Netherfield. Now that her best friend Elizabeth was unavailable, she found that the Dowager's personality and sense of humour was very similar to her friend's.

When she made a comment to that effect, the Dowager responded, 'I always felt that Elizabeth is closest to me of all my granddaughters. We share a very similar outlook on life.'

'A somewhat cynical outlook?' Charlotte asked impertinently, forgetting that she was speaking to the grandmother, not her younger friend.

'I am afraid she learned that from me,' agreed the Dowager. 'I have spent too much time in society to have illusions about their character. There are, of course, wonderful exceptions, but on the whole, I am not impressed.'

'I must admit, unlike my father, I tend to agree with you. I am afraid he is very impressed by rank. Given the slightest opportunity, he cannot stop speaking of St James and all those wonderful nobles he met when he received his knighthood. When I was presented, I met those same nobles and found them rather shallow, to say the least.'

'That is an excellent description of their character,' laughed the Dowager. 'Although I am exceedingly pleased that my daughter and my grandchildren have escaped that fate.'

'Thank you very much, grandmother, for that vote of confidence,' interjected Alistair, who had sat quietly and observed the interaction between his grandmother and Miss Lucas with great interest.

He often let the Dowager carry the conversation so that he could observe Miss Lucas, but at other times he was quite happy to join in.

'I particularly abhor the mercenary way the members of the ton select marriage partners. All they seem to care about is wealth and position. There is often not the slightest consideration whether the couple is in the least compatible. I think that is a most unfortunate state of affairs. What do you think, Miss Lucas?'

'You seem to forget that women have very little say in the matter. Unless they are independently wealthy, women have no choice but to marry since it is almost impossible for them to earn a living. And if they do, they are no longer fit to marry a man of consequence. Not only that, but they have to wait for a man to propose.'

Charlotte smiled a little sadly. 'Most women are grateful if a decent man is prepared to marry them since we are considered almost as property. If a man is vicious, women have no recourse but to endure.'

Alistair was shocked. 'I am sorry, I had not considered it from that perspective. All I saw was that many of the married men of the ton have mistresses. And according to rumour, many of their wives are also finding their own amusements.'

'I gather you object to that kind of behaviour for the women?' Charlotte asked curiously.

'I have an issue with it for both parties,' clarified Alistair, to Charlotte's amazement.

~~DL~~

Charlotte noticed the Duke watching her but thought nothing of it. After all, he was merely being polite and paying attention to the conversation between her and his grandmother.

It did not occur to her that Alistair had no need to even be present. He could have gone off and found other amusements.

But he was intensely interested in what she had to say. The more he heard, the more he liked her.

When they engaged in conversation, she was always polite but not deferential. He found that delightfully refreshing.

One day he could not help but comment on that fact. 'Miss Lucas, I have noticed to my delight that you do not treat me with any more deference than, say, Mr Bennet. Why is that?'

Charlotte laughed, a little embarrassed. 'I suppose it is because the whole town knows of Mrs Bennet's background, even though nobody makes an issue of it. We are aware that she prefers to be known as Mrs Bennet and respect her choice. But Mrs Bennet has been an inspiration to many inhabitants of Meryton.'

Charlotte smiled fondly. 'She is always polite and courteous to everyone, irrespective of their station. We respect her for her behaviour and try to emulate her. I must admit that was one of the problems I had with society in London. Many of the people I met were either fawning toward those of higher station or dismissive if not positively rude to those below. Some of them seem to consider servants to be barely human.'

'You can thank my grandmother for my aunt's attitude. We all learned from her that courtesy costs you nothing but is often well rewarded. Servants, in particular, provide better and more loyal service if you treat them with consideration,' explained Alistair.

'I admit it is good economics. Loyal staff stay in my service, which means we do not have to train new staff. Even though we pay them well, it is still cheaper,' expanded the Dowager.

'I cannot believe that you only act in self-interest and that you do not care for people such as your maid,' cried Charlotte.

'Oh well,' murmured the Dowager almost embarrassed. 'She has been with me for many years, and I have gotten used to her…'

Alistair laughed. 'Grandmother, you may as well admit that you like Julia. I remember Barton that is the Butler at Denton House,' he mentioned as an aside to Charlotte, 'complaining that it was most improper of you to sit with your maid and feed her chicken soup when she was ill.'

'The doctor said she needed to eat, but she refused to accept food from anyone else. She did not dare to refuse me,' the Dowager was adamant.

'Miss Lucas, you mentioned the other day that you have enjoyed reading books about history,' she was determined to change the subject.

Charlotte obliged her by recounting some interesting and amusing facts she had found in those books.

~~DL~~

Charlotte found she liked the Duke. She actually liked him a great deal. But his station was so much above hers that she was certain that he could have no interest in her other than as a friend. Since she was Elizabeth's friend, that was a relationship she could believe in and accept.

Since she was absolutely certain that Alistair could have no other interest in her, she was free to enjoy his company without having to put her best foot forward. She could simply be herself, without worrying that any aspect of her true self would put him off from considering her as a potential marriage prospect.

This certainty made her relaxed and confident and open in a way she had never been before. She did not realise how attractive that made her to a man who had always been subjected to flattery and pretence.

She also did not realise that due to her attitude toward and simple acceptance of him, Alistair relaxed when he was with her.

Other than his friend, Lady Alexandra, who had had no interest in him other than as a friend, Alistair had never met a woman who treated him as a man rather than as a Duke.

He enjoyed their conversations about just about anything, whether trivial or profound. He loved the way her face lit up when discussing her dreams of other countries. When she became animated, she was radiant.

His first impression had been correct. This was a woman who could hold his interest for a lifetime. He was more and more captivated.

~~DL~~

17 Prodigal

At Netherfield, the Bennet and Denton families were having a leisurely breakfast when an unexpected and unannounced visitor strolled into the dining room and gave an elaborate bow to the assembled family members.

'Good morning, grandmother, aunt, uncle, cousins, brother. My timing is perfect, as usual. I see I have arrived just in time for breakfast.' Robert smiled impudently.

Alistair was on his feet and giving his brother a hug before he was even aware that he was moving. 'Robert, where did you come from? What are you doing here? Why did you not write?'

'I gather you missed me?' Robert said while trying to suppress a wince.

Despite his best effort to appear casual, Alistair immediately noticed. 'You are injured.' It was not a question. He looked searchingly at his brother, who gave a slight shrug with his left shoulder. 'Sit down and tell us what happened. I will fix you a plate.'

While Alistair went to the sideboard to get a plate of Robert's favourite foods, Robert greeted his grandmother with a kiss on the cheek. 'Do not worry so much, I am almost completely recovered,' he said with a fond smile.

'Do as you are told. Sit down and tell us what happened to you,' the Dowager ordered. 'Alistair has been fretting.'

Robert took the unoccupied seat next to Lydia. Alistair placed the plate and a cup of coffee before him, then took his own seat again.

Meanwhile, Mrs Bennet signalled a footman to attend her. 'Please arrange for a room in the family wing to be prepared for my nephew.'

Robert had a few bites of his breakfast and took a sip of coffee to wash it down. 'Since you insist on knowing, you now see before you

Colonel Robert Flinter. After that last skirmish I was involved in, they gave me a promotion.'

'If you were *given* a promotion rather than buying it, that must have been quite some skirmish,' opined Mr Bennet.

'It got a bit heated,' admitted Robert. 'Unfortunately, I also ended up with a bullet in my right shoulder. Which is why I did not write. I could not hold a pen for a while. Before you get too worried, the doctors assure me that it will heal completely in time. But it will be a long time before I can be effective with a sword.'

'Does that mean you will retire from the army?' asked his brother hopefully.

'I am afraid I will have to,' Robert replied. 'I already started the process to sell my commission when I got back to town. I invited myself to stay at Denton House. That was also when I found out that you are all at Netherfield and that I just missed Lizzy's wedding by a few days. Did she truly marry that wet blanket Darcy?'

'Yes, she did; but he grows on you when you get to know him. He does have a sense of humour when he relaxes. He is also one of the few men smart enough for our cousin,' Alistair explained.

'And believe it or not, he has some rather radical notions about listening to women,' the Dowager chimed in.

'That is a relief. I like Lizzy, and the usual crowd in London would not suit her,' Robert said with a relieved smile. 'By the way, why are you all at Netherfield, and where is Jane?'

'Did Barton not tell you?' the Dowager asked.

'Tell me what?' asked Robert perplexed. 'You know perfectly well that Barton does not gossip. I practically had to pry the information that you are at Netherfield out of him. Which reminds me, I also borrowed the spare carriage.'

'It was a double wedding. Jane also married.' Alistair deliberately did not provide more information to build up the suspense.

'If Darcy agreed to a double wedding, her husband must be someone he knows well. Are you trying to tell me that she married that puppy Bingley?' Robert was aghast.

'You are worried that Bingley is a puppy but not that he comes from trade?' Mrs Bennet was curious.

'Dear Aunt, being in the army, I have learnt to judge men by their character, not by their antecedents. This may get me burned at the stake amongst the ton, but I would rather follow your example than pander to their fallacious attitude.'

'You can stop worrying. Jane had more sense. She agreed with you and picked a man who liked her for herself and her mind.' Alistair grinned. 'I believe you will approve of her choice.' After a pause, he added, 'Richard Fitzwilliam.'

'What? She married the Colonel?' cried Robert.

'Yes, but he is a Colonel no longer. He also sold his commission to get married,' the Dowager explained.

'It must be a love match because he always said he was looking for an heiress,' Robert grinned.

Mr Bennet laughed. 'It was a love match, but he also married an heiress.'

'No offence, Uncle, but none of your daughters are heiresses unless you have been keeping secrets.'

'Some secrets and a new development. We recently found that there was a codicil in the entailment, which made my cousin Collins ineligible to inherit and made Jane my heir.' Bennet explained.

His wife added, 'Which is why we are all at Netherfield. Thomas handed Longbourn over to Jane and Richard.'

Mrs Bennet looked at her husband and after a moment of silent communication offered, 'you are of course welcome to stay for as long as you like and catch up with your old friend.'

'Thank you, Aunt. After the last few years, it would be nice to have family around.' Now he looked at his cousins and grinned, 'and the view here is much better than it was on the continent.'

Lydia 'accidentally' elbowed him in the ribs. 'I hope your strategy has improved. I need a decent chess partner.'

The Dowager smiled and sighed happily, 'welcome home, grandson.'

~~DL~~

After breakfast, a footman showed Robert to his room, where he found Parker waiting for him.

'When I was informed of your arrival, I took the liberty to unpack your things and had a bath prepared for you, Sir. Would you care for some assistance?'

'You always know what we need. Thank you, Parker.' Now that he was not on display in front of the assembled family, his shoulders slumped, and he winced. 'Yes, I need some assistance. My shoulder still hurts abominably from a bullet wound.'

Parker helped him undress and into the bath. Although he saw the scars, he made no comment other than to say, 'I will return in half an hour.'

Robert was grateful for the heat of the bath and the solitude. Although he had had both at Denton House, he felt like an intruder there, even though he had effectively grown up in that house, but the silence weighed on him. Here at Netherfield, his family made a pleasant background noise of barely heard conversation.

He realised that the silence at Denton House had reminded him too much of the tense silence on the battlefield just before all hell broke loose. It had made him apprehensive. Without realising it at the time, he had expected an ambush, a fight, horrendous mayhem, the kind that had been giving him nightmares while he was in hospital.

Nightmares about friends and comrades dying, and even worse of being injured and screaming at him to save them. At least the dead were silent.

But now he was amongst family again. He hoped that with their unwitting support, his nightmares would go away.

He was in two minds about having Richard Fitzwilliam nearby. He liked and respected the man tremendously, but he hoped that Richard would not want to relive old battles. Robert had had a lifetime's worth of them and wanted nothing so much as to forget them.

~~DL~~

Over the next few days, Robert relaxed into a family life he had never truly known. He was surrounded by a happy, noisy family. Not that any one of them was particularly noisy, but there were so many family members. He was astonished how welcoming and restful it was.

The rest and the relaxing atmosphere did wonders for Robert's shoulder as well. It still twinged occasionally, but he could perform most actions without problems.

His situation became even more relaxing after the first visit of Richard Fitzwilliam. After welcoming Robert enthusiastically, he quietly asked, 'Robert, how do you feel about your time in the army?'

'It was gratifying serving my country, but now I have no wish to be reminded of the horrors I witnessed,' was Robert's equally quiet reply.

'Thank god. I was afraid that you might be one of those benighted chaps who revel in the glory of war. Which is something I now prefer to forget. I am pleased we understand each other.' Richard smiled before he turned his attention to the other conversation going on around them.

~~DL~~

Robert noticed that Miss Charlotte Lucas was a frequent visitor. Admittedly she was friendly with all the Bennet ladies and had been adopted by his grandmother, but during each of her visits, Alistair was invariably present as well.

When he started paying attention, it became obvious to him that something was developing between Alistair and Miss Lucas. The way each of them would look at the other when they thought the other was not looking, spoke volumes to Robert.

One evening, when they were having a final brandy before bed, he broached the subject. 'I have noticed that you pay a great deal of attention to Miss Lucas.'

'You have? I thought only grandmother knew,' responded a startled Alistair.

'Since I am neither blind, deaf or simple, yes, I have noticed.' Robert grinned at his brother.

'Do you think anyone else in the family has noticed?' Alistair was concerned.

'That depends. How many of your family members are blind, deaf and simple?' Robert teased. When Alistair looked uncomfortable, he continued, 'but I have also noticed that they are exceedingly careful *not* to notice.'

Alistair still looked embarrassed. 'I am trying to get to know the lady. Having mistaken Lady Francesca's inclinations and motives, I am more cautious now.' He sighed. 'But Miss Lucas intrigues me, and I cannot seem to stay away. At the moment I am looking forward to the assembly next week when I will have a chance to dance with her.'

'How many dances are you planning on?' asked Robert, who started to grin as an idea came to him.

'I am planning to request the first and the supper sets,' admitted Alistair. 'Any more would raise too many expectations amongst her family and friends.'

'Do you remember when at all those assemblies I pretended to be you?'

'Yes, I do, and I was very grateful, but that will not be necessary this time.'

'I was not going to suggest that. I thought you might like to pretend to be me, at least for part of the evening. Say for two sets that your brother has requested of the lady?' Robert grinned mischievously.

'That would be a most scandalous deception,' said Alistair severely before breaking into a wide grin.

Robert added his carefree laugh. 'I see we still think alike.'

~~DL~~

The evening of the assembly, the Dowager looked suspiciously at her grandsons. 'To the best of my knowledge, which is extensive, this is the first time ever that you two did not dress identically to go to an assembly. What are you planning?'

'We are not planning anything, grandmother,' replied Robert, who was wearing a blue coat, with an innocent mien.

Alistair, wearing a green coat, chimed in, 'It is simply that we both have requested dances with Miss Lucas, and it simply would not do to have people think that one of us was dancing more than two sets with the lady.'

'Of course not,' agreed the Dowager blandly. 'We would not want people to think that one of you had serious intentions toward Miss Lucas. Even dancing two sets is a mark of significant favour. I expect Miss Lucas is going to be very tired by the end of the evening.'

The Dowager's prediction came true. The other gentlemen also noticed that the supposed spinster was opening the assembly with the most eligible man present and were quick to request the other available dances. Charlotte did not sit out a single dance for the entire evening.

Lady Lucas was astonished that both of Elizabeth's cousins had singled out her daughter for two sets each, but she was exceedingly pleased that this favour encouraged other single gentlemen to dance with Charlotte.

Maybe there was hope yet, and Charlotte would attract one of those gentlemen to consider her as a wife. Not the two lords of course, but one of the local gentlemen.

In the meantime, Alistair thoroughly enjoyed all his dances with the lady. Charlotte was rather confused once she realised that her dance partner was Alistair rather than Robert.

When she called him out on his deceptions, Alistair smiled impishly and explained, 'Robert is still injured and cannot dance as much as he should, but it is acceptable for each of us to sit out two sets. I am simply covering for him.'

'You could have taken two of his other dances,' suggested Charlotte.

'I could have, but I prefer to dance with you rather than my cousins,' replied Alistair with fake innocence.

Considering how much she enjoyed her dances with this particular gentleman, Charlotte decided not to argue.

~~DL~~

18 Proposal

Alistair, the Duke of Denton, came to a decision. He was going to propose marriage to the lovely Miss Charlotte Lucas.

Admittedly, her connections and dowry were minor, but that was more than made up by the fact that she was a gentlewoman, kind and intelligent, graceful, and gracious, and he liked and respected her. In addition, and he only admitted this fact to himself, he found that even just thinking of her made his body respond in the most delightful way.

Apart from that, he enjoyed her company to the point that he wanted that company on a permanent basis.

He felt very protective of her. He had realised that, as he became angry when he heard someone sneer at the fact that she was a spinster.

Yes, it was time that he made his intentions clear.
~~DL~~
Alistair took his stallion, Perseus, for a ride towards Meryton. He left his horse at a nearby stable and walked to Lucas Lodge.

Miss Lucas was at home, but amenable to go for a stroll with Alistair.

They chatted about inconsequential things until Alistair gathered his courage and asked, 'Miss Lucas, do you believe in love at first sight?'

'No, Your Grace, I do not. I am not certain I believe in love at all.' Charlotte smiled sadly. 'At least for myself. I have always been too practical. Unlike Elizabeth, who always insisted she would only marry for love. But she could afford to be particular.'

'You have never been in love?' Alistair persisted.

'No, I have never before met a man who inspired that kind of a feeling in me,' Charlotte declared.

While the statement was true, it was also misleading. Charlotte had never been in love before. But she was in love now, and she knew it was hopeless.

It was ridiculous that at her age she had developed a passion for a very particular man. No, to be completely truthful she had fallen head over heels in love with the man addressing her now.

Since they had met for Lizzy's wedding, she had spent what seemed an inordinate amount of time in his company. His manner towards her was exquisite.

They discussed many subjects, and he always listened to her. She felt that he respected her and her opinions. They might argue a point, but when he disagreed with her, it was always well reasoned. Sometimes, when she convinced him to change his opinion, he never seemed to begrudge her having won the argument.

He never once gave the impression that he expected her to agree with him, just because she was a woman. Or because he was a man and a noble to boot. This was a novelty to her.

It also did not hurt that he was handsome and had a sly sense of humour.

But he could never be interested in her due to her status, the daughter of a very minor knight; her dowry, which was virtually non-existent; her age, at seven and twenty she was very much on the shelf; and her looks, which were plain at best.

But she was determined to enjoy his company as a friend for as long as possible.

'I admit, I am grateful for that. Considering how plain I am, I would have ended up in that unpalatable situation of unrequited love. No man wants a plain wife when he can have a beautiful one.'

'What makes you think you are plain?' Alistair was shocked.

'My mother has been bemoaning that fact ever since I can remember. Almost everyone tells me so. Except Eliza. Generous soul that she is, she tries to tell me I am beautiful. But she is biased by our friendship.'

'I hate to disagree with you and your mother, but Lizzy is correct. You are lovely.' When Charlotte tried to deny his assertion, he continued, 'yours may not be a classically beautiful face, but you are a striking looking woman.'

Now he grinned. 'You have met Richard's mother. Would you say she is beautiful?'

'Yes, of course. She looks stunning,' exclaimed Charlotte.

'You obviously did not look at her closely. Your face is much more symmetrical and delicate than hers. But because of how she carries herself and her personality, people never really notice that she looks like a horse. And please do not ever tell her I said so.' Alistair looked beseechingly at Charlotte. 'She would flay me with her tongue.'

He shrugged. 'But to get back to the point, her vivacity makes her appear more beautiful than her physical beauty. I admit that I am no expert on lady's fashions, but the way she dresses and moves makes an impact. So, despite the fact that she looks like a horse, everyone sees her as stunning.'

'But I am not vivacious as she is,' Charlotte protested.

'No, yours is a more quiet beauty, but it is beauty nonetheless.'

Charlotte shook her head. Although she wanted to deny it, Alistair's impassioned speech made her feel like maybe she was not quite as plain as she had been taught to believe. But it was irrelevant. At her age, she knew that no man would want to marry her unless he was desperate.

Therefore, she was shocked when she heard the Duke say, 'You are also intelligent, kind, gentle and compassionate. You are not impressed by my wealth and my title, which I find wonderfully refreshing. Because of that and much more, I find myself head over heels in love with you.'

Alistair paused for a moment before he asked, 'would you make me the happiest of men and become my wife?'

Charlotte stared at him for a long minute before whispering, 'I cannot.'

~~DL~~

Alistair, who had thought that Charlotte cared for him, or at least liked him, was confused and as shocked by her answer as she had been by his question.

'But why?' he blurted out at last. 'I thought you liked me, at least a little. I can offer you a good home as well as love and respect. I am generally thought to be a good catch. Please tell me why you cannot marry me.'

'You are all that and more. I cannot tell you why, but I cannot marry you.' Charlotte had turned pale as the enormity of the situation sank in. 'I am sorry.'

With those words she rushed off, leaving a completely bewildered Duke standing forlorn on the path.

~~DL~~

You fool, Charlotte berated herself. *You are in love with a wonderful man, who is not only kind and intelligent but also handsome, wealthy and a Duke no less. He also says he loves you AND YOU REFUSE HIS PROPOSAL? Are you out of your mind? For years you promised yourself that if a respectable man asks for your hand, you would accept. Now this decent man asks you to marry him, and you say no. What is wrong with you? Why did you say no?*

Charlotte carried on in this vein for quite half an hour before she calmed down enough to actually think about the questions, she was asking herself.

What is wrong with him that has you turning down the most eligible man you are ever likely to meet?

He loves you.

He thinks you are beautiful.

He is handsome.

He has a wonderful family.

Eliza would be your cousin by marriage.

He is intelligent.

He is kind.

He is considerate.

He is respectful.

He is wealthy.

He is a Duke. *Dear Lord in heaven. He is a DUKE. He wants to make me his Duchess. There is no way that I can be a duchess. I would make a complete fool of myself in his society. Those sharks would eat me alive.*

Charlotte remembered Mrs Bennet's comments about London society. The jockeying for position. The snide remarks. The vicious and malicious gossip.

They would have a field day sniping at the little country spinster who had snared the most eligible Duke. They would assume a compromise and spread the most vile gossip. No, it was too much.

She would not be the fodder of the disapprobation of the whole society. She simply could not do it.

~~DL~~

19 Family Council

At long last Alistair gathered his wits and went to collect his horse. On his return to Netherfield, he remained deep in thought.

Why had Charlotte rejected his proposal? He had been certain that she cared for him. Even if she did not love him as much as he loved her, any sensible woman would have accepted his hand. After all, he had an enviable position in society, he was wealthy, intelligent, courteous, honourable, and even he had to admit that he was passably good looking. He was certainly in good shape with all the exercise he was getting.

Why was that not enough for Miss Lucas? Had he said something wrong? He could not make head or tail of it. It was going to drive him to drink.

Even riding slowly, he eventually arrived back at Netherfield. He handed the reins of Perseus to a groom in an abstracted manner and went into the house.

He thought about going to his room but thought that a book might distract him from his thoughts. He was so focused on his intent when entering the library that he did not notice Mr Bennet.

His uncle looked up from his own book and noticed the abstraction about Alistair. 'What is the matter, nephew? You left the house this morning in high spirits, and now you look as if your favourite horse had died. Since I saw you riding Perseus not five minutes ago, I know that is not the case. Therefore, something else troubles you.'

Without thinking of guarding his tongue, Alistair said, 'Miss Lucas declined my proposal.'

'Did she now? I wonder why.'

'I do not know. She only said she cannot marry me,' Alistair said in a deflated voice.

'What will you do now? Will you accept her choice, or will you try to change her mind?'

'How can I decide when I do not know why she refused.'

Bennet looked thoughtful for a minute before he suggested, 'it takes a female mind to understand a female mind. My wife may be able to shed some light on Miss Lucas' decision.'

'I had not thought of that,' Alistair exclaimed. 'I must go and ask her.'

'Wait. I will ask her to join us. We have more privacy here unless you are prepared to involve the whole family.' When Alistair hesitated, his uncle continued, 'I am certain all my ladies would like to help. But it is your pride which might suffer.'

'More than it already has suffered? But it might be wise to ask Aunt Francine if she can shed some light on my conundrum. If she cannot assist, then we can still ask the rest of the family.'

'Well said, nephew.' Mr Bennet rang the bell. When a footman responded, he requested, 'Could you please ask Mrs Bennet if she has time to join us?'

When Mrs Bennet arrived, her husband laid the problem before her and asked her views.

Mrs Bennet was as puzzled as the gentlemen. 'I thought Charlotte head over heels in love with you. I cannot fathom why she would refuse.'

'You think she loves me?' Alistair asked hopefully.

'I thought so, which makes her refusal even more confusing. I simply cannot make it out.' Mrs Bennet shook her head. 'Jane and Richard have just arrived. She knows Charlotte better than anyone except for Lizzy. Maybe she can guess Charlotte's reasons.'

Alistair took a deep breath and straightened up. 'My pride be damned. I need answers. Let us consult with the family.'

~~DL~~

Mr and Mrs Bennet led Alistair to the drawing-room where the whole family had gathered to chat with Jane and Richard.

The newcomers greeted Jane and Richard before settling into seats. After some general conversation, Mrs Bennet broached the subject of

Charlotte. 'I had some surprising news. It appears Charlotte rejected a proposal, and I was wondering why she would do such a thing?'

Jane immediately responded, 'she would not unless the man could not provide her with a home, or he is known to be vicious.'

'If he is kind, intelligent, personable and well off?' prompted her mother.

'Then she would accept,' Jane stated with certainty.

'If he is a kind man, can you think of any reason why she would refuse a proposal?'

'Maybe if he is not vicious but had a bad reputation?' Jane speculated. 'She always said she wanted to marry a respectable man.'

'If there is nothing wrong with the man other than the usual silliness that he may be too sure of himself?'

'Then, she would not refuse.'

'If Charlotte would not refuse such a man, what would make you refuse him?' asked Mrs Bennet, looking around the room at her other daughters.

'Because I did not love him,' was Kitty's answer

'Because I could not like or respect him,' supplied Mary.

'He has a ghastly family,' Lydia opined.

'There is a vast difference in position,' Jane suggested.

'Why would a vast difference in position be an issue to you?' asked Richard.

'Because neither of us would fit into the other's world.'

'Could not the lower-ranked person learn to fit in?' Richard suggested. 'I have seen it often enough. Second sons marrying heiresses who were the daughters of tradesmen. The ladies were usually only too happy to learn.'

'I would not marry a man if I were in love with someone else,' Mary quietly ventured another opinion.

'That must be it. The reason Charlotte rejected a proposal.' Lydia looked excited. She turned to Alistair, who had been sitting quietly while listening to the ladies' speculations. 'Sorry cousin, I do not wish to make you uncomfortable, but I am certain Charlotte is in love with you.' She turned back to address the rest of the group.

'That is why Charlotte would reject a proposal. She cannot marry someone else while she is in love with Alistair.' Lydia looked triumphant for having proposed the solution to the puzzle.

Alistair said quietly, 'mine was the proposal she rejected.' His statement was received with stunned disbelief.

'She shows some sense,' was Richard's sly comment, which earned him angry glares from all the women in the room.

Robert commented, 'I have heard of many women who are reluctant to be spinsters, but I have never before heard of a woman who was reluctant to be a Duchess.'

Mrs Bennet looked around the room, but no one seemed to have an answer to Alistair's predicament.

'Since we cannot help, we will have to wait a couple of days,' Mrs Bennet said at last. 'Lizzy and William will arrive then. If she cannot give you an answer, she will ask Charlotte herself.'

Alistair had to be content with that.

~~DL~~

For the next two days, Alistair found excuses to visit Lucas Lodge, but Charlotte was never 'home'. At last, the anxiously anticipated couple arrived.

Darcy was shocked to hear that Alistair had proposed to Charlotte.

'Alistair, why would you want to marry the daughter of a minor knight? You can choose any woman to be your wife. I cannot think of any single woman in our circles who would refuse you.'

Alistair shot back. 'You proposed to Lizzy even though you thought she was the penniless daughter of a minor country gentleman. Why should I not wish to marry the daughter of a minor country knight? Apart from that, since I outrank the majority of people in this country, my wife would almost certainly be of a lower station before our marriage. Therefore, her initial rank is irrelevant.'

Darcy was startled to be reminded of his own misguided opinions. Both that he considered rank as a major factor in the choice of wife and how badly he had misjudged the Bennets. 'I wish you had not reminded me of my stupidity. But Elizabeth was in love with me, and she said yes.'

'Would you have simply given up if Lizzy had said no? Or would you have tried to change her mind?'

'Touché. I would have fought for her love.'

Elizabeth, on the other hand, had no problem with her cousin wanting to marry her best friend.

She was shocked to hear that Charlotte had refused. 'I cannot think of a single reason why she would not marry you,' she declared.

'Charlotte always prided herself on being pragmatic. She was prepared to marry any respectable man who could provide her with a home of her own so that she would not be a burden on her family any longer. Her refusal is totally out of character.'

She looked at Alistair quizzically. 'You did not by chance insult her by pointing out your difference in stations, and that she should be grateful, you deigned to even consider someone as lowly.'

'No, of course not. I did not even consider her station. I did mention that I thought it wonderful that she was the only woman who is not impressed by *my* wealth and station. But I never even implied that she was in any way inferior.' He ran his hand through his hair as if he were trying to tear it out.

'In that case, I simply do not understand Charlotte's reasoning. Therefore, the only thing to do is for me to ask her myself.'
~~DL~~
Elizabeth returned from her visit with Charlotte the following afternoon.

'I am sorry, Cousin. I am none the wiser. Charlotte simply says she cannot marry you. I could not get her to disclose her reason.' Lizzy sighed. 'I wanted to shake her to make her tell me, but she looked so sad that I could not do it.'

Alistair gave Elizabeth a hug. 'Thank you for trying.'
~~DL~~
Elizabeth and Darcy left with Georgiana for London the following day.

The younger girls all missed their new friend, but Lydia, in particular, was desolate.

Mrs Bennet had a quiet chat with her youngest daughter. 'Lydia, I know you miss Georgiana. But you will see her again for Christmas.'

'I will?' Lydia squealed in excited surprise.

'You will. In the meantime, William wanted his immediate family to have a chance to become a family. Give Georgiana and Lizzy a chance to get to know each other better. I hope you can be patient for a little while.'

Lydia sighed, 'I will try. I cannot promise, but I will try.'

Mrs Bennet laughed as she gave her daughter a hug. 'That is all I ask for.'

~~DL~~

Alistair moped around the house for another couple of days and not even his brother could cheer him up.

'I need to speak to her, but I cannot force the issue because her parents could find out that I proposed, and they might try to force her to accept. I do not wish for her to be pressured. I want her to be happy with whatever choice she makes.'

Robert suggested, 'give her time. She might change her mind.'

~~DL~~

20 Big Guns

During all those discussions and speculations, only one person had kept her own counsel. She now decided the situation warranted her interference. In other words, to use one of Robert's metaphors, it was time to bring in the big guns.

The Dowager Duchess made a morning call at Lucas Lodge. Lady Lucas, although a little flustered at the unexpected visitor, rose to the occasion and offered refreshments, which were graciously accepted.

They had a pleasant chat about nothing in particular while they drank their tea.

'Miss Lucas, on my way in, I noticed you have a rather pretty garden. Would you care to take a stroll since the weather is remarkably fine today?' asked the Dowager.

'I would be delighted to show you our garden, Your Grace,' replied Charlotte nervously. She suspected this stroll had been the purpose of this visit.

They collected their bonnets, gloves, and parasols before making their way into the garden.

When they were far enough away from the house not to be overheard, the Dowager addressed Charlotte, 'Miss Lucas, you can be in no doubt as to the reason for my visit.'

'I would not presume to speculate on the intentions of your actions, Your Grace,' Charlotte tried to prevaricate.

'Come now, Miss Lucas, you are aware from your friendship with Elizabeth that we are a tight-knit family. Popular custom to the contrary we actually confide in each other when something troubles us.'

The Dowager sighed, 'Miss Lucas, I shall be frank with you, and I sincerely hope that you shall do me the same courtesy.' She cocked an eyebrow at Charlotte, who smiled at the familiar gesture from this not so familiar and rather intimidating woman.

When she observed the smile, the Dowager nodded in satisfaction. 'Good. I see you are going to be sensible. I require an explanation why you refused my grandson's proposal. My grandson Alistair,' she emphasised.

Charlotte turned serious again and sighed. 'Your Grace, your grandson could have any suitable woman he desires. I do not think that I am suitable for him.'

'Explain further if you please.'

'Lord Denton should have a wife who is beautiful, wealthy and titled. That is what is expected of him by society.'

'You are wealthy enough for Alistair since he has more money than he knows what to do with, your father has a title, and you are beautiful. Certainly, more so than the Countess of Matlock. Try again.'

'I am a spinster. I am on the shelf. If he marries me, everyone will assume that I compromised him,' Charlotte protested.

'Only if you marry quickly and from obscurity.' The Dowager sighed again. 'You have not mentioned the most important aspect. Do you care for him?'

Charlotte blushed and looked down on her hands which were gripping her parasol so tightly that her knuckles were white. 'Yes, I do,' she whispered.

'If you are turning him down because you are too afraid to stand up for yourself, then he is better off without you. But if you truly care for him, you will face the harpies of the *ton*. Just keep in mind, you do not have to do it alone. You will have support from the families.'

Charlotte looked up at the Dowager with surprise at those words. After a moment, the surprise turned to embarrassment. 'I had not considered that I would have support. I expected to flounder around and be an embarrassment to Lord Denton. He deserves better than that.'

'So he does. But that is a problem that can be fixed with some education and the support of friends and family.' Now the Dowager smiled. She was relieved that Charlotte's reasons were born of concern for her grandson rather than cowardice, or worse, indifference.

She now became all brisk efficiency. 'Very well, Miss Lucas, we shall make this work. There is much to do. First, we have to make you look like a potential Duchess. Tomorrow you will come to London with me, where we will commission a new wardrobe.'

When Charlotte looked like she wanted to protest, the Dowager silenced her with a look. 'Although we will not make the engagement public just yet, that is my engagement present to you. Then your education will begin. I will teach you how to deal with those harpies.'

The Dowager patted Charlotte's hands. 'Now be a dear and start packing.'

~~DL~~

Charlotte had gone to do her packing while the Dowager returned to the parlour to speak to Lady Lucas.

'My dear Lady Lucas, I must confess to a small deception. I find that I need to return to London for a fortnight or so. But I do not like travelling without the company of a lady with whom I can have a conversation to distract me from the rigours of the journey. Since I have become rather fond of your daughter, I was hoping to invite her to accompany me. To my delight, she has agreed, provided you have no objections.' The Dowager smiled her best charming smile.

Lady Lucas was astonished but thrilled that her spinster daughter had the opportunity to accompany the Dowager. At best, Charlotte might have the opportunity to meet and attract an eligible man. At worst, she would have an enjoyable visit in London. Somewhere in between was also the possibility that the Dowager was considering Charlotte as her companion. The first and last options were the best since that would relieve the family of the financial burden of supporting the young woman.

Lady Lucas happily agreed to the scheme. 'Your Grace, since you find Charlotte to be congenial company, I am pleased to have her accompany you wherever you wish to go. I am certain she will be in the safest possible hands.'

'I am gratified that you are agreeable to the scheme, especially since it is on such short notice. Please tell Miss Lucas that I will collect her at nine o'clock tomorrow. Now I must be off to supervise my own packing. Good day to you, Lady Lucas.'

~~DL~~

As soon as the Dowager returned to Netherfield, she started giving orders. 'Mrs Nicholls, please instruct my maid to pack some trunks for me for a two week stay in London. I will need an early breakfast tomorrow as I instructed my coachman that I will be leaving at half-past eight. Now, where might I find Lord Denton?'

'Lord Denton is in the library with Mr Bennet, Your Grace. I will pass on your orders now.' Mrs Nicholls curtsied to carry out her orders. As usual, she forgot that the Dowager was not technically the mistress of the estate anymore.

Meanwhile, the Dowager made her way to the library. 'Thomas, Alistair,' she acknowledged the men seated at the chessboard.

They politely rose and greeted her as 'Mother' and Grandmother' respectively.

'Alistair, you will be pleased to know that I will be leaving for London tomorrow,' she informed her grandson.

'But what about my little problem?' he queried.

'Your problem will accompany me.' She smirked. 'But you had better find a more suitable nickname for your intended. I do not think she would appreciate being called "Problem", not even the diminutive "Little Problem".'

The stunned look on Alistair's face caused his grandmother to chuckle.

'Intended! Are you telling me that five minutes conversation with you has changed her mind?' Although Alistair was delighted, he was also a little put off that his grandmother had succeeded where he had failed.

'She was only afraid that she was not good enough for you and that you deserved better. She also had not realised that she would not have to face the harpies on her own. Foolish girl. But young women in love do not usually think logically.'

The Dowager smiled fondly at her grandson. 'I believe she is as besotted with you as you are with her. But,' she said as Alistair looked as if he would rush to Charlotte's side, 'you will need to practice some

116

patience and show a lot of restraint. We have some battles before us to win society over to her side.'

'I want to speak to her.' Alistair started to look mulish.

'So you shall, but not today. She is busy packing for her trip to London with me tomorrow. If you promise to behave yourself, you may accompany us.'

A quiet chuckle alerted the two that they were not alone in the room. Bennet had settled back into his chair and listened avidly. 'You poor boy, having to be patient and restrained. That is what you get for not being a commoner. Console yourself, it's a Duke's life, but someone has to do it. '

~~DL~~

At eight o'clock the following morning, Alistair was packed, dressed, had breakfasted and was ready to leave when his grandmother walked into the dining room for her own breakfast.

While she had a leisurely meal, Alistair started pacing.

'If you cannot sit still, take your pacing elsewhere. You are spoiling my enjoyment of the meal. And I will not be rushed, no matter how impatient you are,' the Dowager admonished her grandson.

Alistair bowed sarcastically. 'I shall take my pacing outside and shall *patiently* await you.'

'Thank you. I appreciate your consideration.' The Dowager smiled impishly while continuing her meal.

She and her maid stepped outside the front door with one minute to spare off the appointed time.

The carriage was waiting, the step was in place, and Alistair stood ready to hand her and the maid into the carriage.

Once they were all settled, the Dowager in the forward-facing seat while her companions sat opposite, the carriage took off towards Meryton.

'When we get to Lucas Lodge, you will remain in the carriage,' instructed the Dowager. 'I am certain that you can remain patient for five more minutes. If you try to leave the carriage, Julia has instructions to sit on your lap. Since I presume you would not wish Miss Lucas to find you in that position, I expect you to behave.'

'Yes, grandmother. I will be good,' Alistair acquiesced.

~~DL~~

21 Plans

When the Dowager arrived at Lucas Lodge, Sir William Lucas was almost beside himself at the honour the lady was bestowing on his daughter, to ask for her company.

'Sir William, please calm yourself. Miss Lucas is graciously agreeing to be my guest. The pleasure of her company is all mine,' the Dowager stemmed the flow of Sir William's expostulation by adding, 'but we simply must be going, while the weather is still cool enough for the horses.'

The Dowager's footmen were on hand to assist first Charlotte and then the Dowager into the carriage, giving Sir William and Lady Lucas no option other than to stand back.

As soon as they were settled, the carriage took off. The Dowager heaved a sigh of relief. 'That went better than I had hoped for.' She turned to Charlotte. 'I really did not wish to explain my grandson's presence,' she said with her impish smile.

Charlotte was a little flustered. The last time she had seen the Duke, she had declined his proposal. Now that she had effectively accepted it via the Dowager, she felt rather embarrassed.

The Dowager cut through the confusion, 'children, as soon as we get to London, you can speak privately and resolve any outstanding questions. In the meantime, we need to make some plans.'

'When we get to London, we will first go to Darcy House. I sent an express to Elizabeth informing her that she has invited you, Charlotte, to be her guest for the next few weeks.'

When Alistair tried to object, she explained, 'propriety must be observed. It would not do to have you both stay under the same roof for the moment.'

Alistair grudgingly agreed.

'For Charlotte to stay with the Darcys has two other advantages. One, she is Elizabeth's dearest friend, and it is only natural for Elizabeth to invite her to visit. Two, Elizabeth will also require a new wardrobe. Therefore, it is logical for both ladies to visit the modistes together. Also, quite naturally, since Elizabeth is my granddaughter, I will have every reason to accompany them.'

'Did you say modistes, as in plural?' Charlotte asked, shocked.

'Of course, plural. It would not do to get too many dresses from a single outfitter. They would wonder why someone needs a complete wardrobe.'

Alistair looked at Charlotte with sympathy. 'It has been said that my grandmother would have made a wonderful general.'

'So I am starting to learn.' Charlotte looked worried.

The Dowager gently patted her hand. 'Cheer up, my dear. It will not be nearly as bad as you imagine.'

Alistair just rolled his eyes before giving Charlotte an encouraging smile.

'Now, the rest of our campaign. Once you are appropriately outfitted, we will call on friends, Countess Matlock, Lady Worthington, Lady Sefton...'

'You should include Countess Marven,' suggested Alistair.

'She would be a good choice, but I only know her as a passing acquaintance.'

'As it happens, she and I have been friends for the last decade.' Alistair grinned at his grandmother's surprised look.

'Why did you not mention this before. I hear she has a delightful niece, who is now married.'

'That is exactly why I did not mention my friendship with Lady Beatrice and Alexandra. Alexandra is more like a sister to me.' Alistair addressed Charlotte, 'I must introduce you to Lady Alexandra. I believe you two can be good friends.'

'Oh dear, what did I agree to?'

'You agreed to be educated in the ways of the *ton*. Which we will do while you wait for your new wardrobe. Then you will experience it at first hand. Initially, in the company of people who I know will support you. When you become more comfortable with our friends, we will visit the theatre and the opera. I hope you like music,' the Dowager was in full flight.

Charlotte had barely time to say, 'I love music,' before the Dowager continued.

'Excellent, at least you will enjoy the music. I think we will have the Fitzwilliams accompany us to the theatre with Darcy and Elizabeth.'

'Once we have established you as a friend of Lizzy's, visiting from the country, Alistair can start to officially court you.'

Alistair nearly choked at the cavalier way his grandmother was ordering his life. Now it was Charlotte's turn to roll her eyes and give him an encouraging smile.

They spent the rest of the journey discussing the Dowagers plans in more detail.

~~DL~~

When the Denton carriage pulled up in front of Darcy House, they were expected.

Elizabeth and Darcy gave the visitors a few minutes to refresh themselves before they all were supposed to meet for tea and more discussions.

Alistair was waiting when the Dowager and Charlotte came down the stairs again.

'We are at Darcy House. I would like to speak with Miss Lucas in private for a few moments,' he addressed his grandmother in a rather challenging tone, before turning to Charlotte with a charming smile. 'Would you please allow me to speak to you for a moment in private?'

'I would like that,' replied Charlotte.

'You may use the library,' the Dowager offered.

'I think the morning room would be safer. You never know what you might find in the library when Darcy and Elizabeth are around,' quipped Alistair before leading Charlotte to the indicated room.

The left the door open but moved to the far side of the room for maximum privacy.

'Miss Lucas, although I am thrilled that you have come here, I would like to be certain it is of your own free will. My grandmother can be rather overwhelming and is used to getting her way. She did not bully you, I hope?'

'I suppose, you could say that she bullied me,' Charlotte smiled when Alistair looked worried, 'but only into giving her my reasons for declining your offer.'

'Would you tell me your reasons, please?' Alistair requested.

Charlotte sighed, 'I am not used to the kind of society in which you move. I was afraid that I would embarrass you. To my mind, you deserve the very best, and I thought you could do so very much better than myself.'

Charlotte swallowed convulsively before straightening, and she admitted, 'I was also afraid. Afraid that people would think that the only way you would marry someone like me was that I compromised you. I did not think I could deal with that kind of gossip. I admit I panicked and did not even consider that I would have the support of your family.'

'Of course, you will have the support of our families. Never doubt that,' exclaimed Alister. He continued more softly, 'but does that mean that you are now prepared to make me the happiest of men?' He reached out his hand in an invitation for Charlotte to take.

Charlotte looked into his eyes, then down at the proffered hand. When she looked back into Alistair's eyes, she smiled while she took his hand and simply said, 'yes.'

'Thank you.' Alistair raised her hand to his lips for a featherlight kiss on her bare skin. Charlotte gave a small gasp at the sensation he had caused.

They stood looking at each other for a minute until they were interrupted by someone clearing their throat.

When they turned toward the door, the Dowager smiled and said, 'Lizzy and William are waiting.'

~~DL~~

Charlotte entered the drawing-room on Alistair's arm following the

Dowager. Elizabeth and Darcy looked up at their entrance.

Elizabeth smiled at Charlotte. 'I assume since you arrived together, you have managed to overcome your reservations?'

'Her Grace can be most persuasive,' replied Charlotte.

'Please call me grandmother when in private. In public, Lady Amelia will do,' the Dowager offered with a smile. 'To quote Alistair, I am tired of being graced to death.'

'Thank you, grandmother. As long as you do me the honour and call me Charlotte,' the lady answered with a happy smile. It seemed all of Lord Denton's, no she must remember to think of him as Alistair. All of Alistair's family seemed to approve of the match.

'How soon will I be able to call you Cousin?' Lizzy wanted to know.

'It will be several months, depending on how quickly we can get Charlotte established in society,' answered the Dowager in Charlotte's stead.

'We are happy to host you for as long as you need,' Darcy offered.

'Thank you, Mr Darcy, you are most kind,' responded Charlotte.

'Under the circumstances, you had better call me William, Cousin to be,' grinned the gentleman.

'It will be my pleasure, William.'

'Now, can we get down to business. My aching bones need a hot bath,' the Dowager cut short the pleasantries.

'I presume you have a plan, grandmother,' stated Elizabeth.

'First of all, we need to make Charlotte look like a potential duchess. That means a new wardrobe. You said you would need to shop for a new wardrobe for yourself, Lizzy.'

When Elizabeth agreed, the Dowager continued. 'Charlotte will stay here as your guest. When you go shopping, she will accompany you and acquire a new wardrobe at the same time. I will join you as well since it has been some time since I significantly updated my own wardrobe.'

'Once she looks the part, you and Charlotte and I will go visiting. We will also go to the theatre and possibly to Almack's. In a few weeks,

Alistair will officially start courting your friend. By that time nobody should question his choice.'

'We can work out further details tomorrow after I have rested,' the Dowager finished her instructions.

'You are still the strategist, I see,' complimented Darcy.

'Everyone needs an interest,' the lady agreed with a smug smile.

~~DL~~

22 Education

The following morning the Dowager arrived at Darcy House at the most unfashionable hour of half-past eight. She was immediately shown into the dining room, where the Darcys and Charlotte were having breakfast.

'Good morning, I am happy to see that you are keeping country hours,' she greeted the family.

'Good morning, grandmother. Please have a seat. If you would like some breakfast, I will fix you a plate,' offered Darcy.

'Thank you, that would be lovely,' the Dowager accepted.

While Darcy put together a plate of food, Elizabeth told her grandmother, 'I received a note from Aunt Susan yesterday. She decided that I need assistance in selecting a new wardrobe. I believe she wants to ensure that I do not stint on the number of outfits I plan to purchase. She will be here in half an hour.'

'Excellent. She has exquisite taste. I will admit I have not paid a great deal of attention to fashion in recent years,' admitted the Dowager. 'Since I know which styles and colours suit me, I tend to stay away from the more extreme trends. It will be good to have Susan with us.'

'I am glad you feel this way, Amelia,' came Lady Susan's comment as she entered the room. 'Good morning, everyone.' She then noticed Charlotte. 'Good morning, Miss Lucas. I was not aware you are in town.'

'Good morning, Susan. You are just in time to help us with a special project,' Amelia smiled her usual impish smile.

'I am happy to help. What is the special project?'

'We need to make Charlotte look like a duchess.' The Dowager chuckled at the stunned look on Lady Susan's face.

After a minute's thought, the lady broke into a wide smile and said, 'Alistair, of course.' She then addressed Charlotte, 'you will make a wonderful addition to our families.'

'I presume this is not official until Miss Lucas is firmly established in society?' she asked the Dowager.

'You are as perceptive as ever.'

'That changes my plan. I had intended for Elizabeth to get most of her wardrobe from my favourite modiste. But since we cannot make it too obvious that Miss Lucas is getting a complete wardrobe, we will need to spread our purchases over several modistes.'

She thought a moment. 'Yes, that will work, since we are now getting dresses for two ladies...'

The Dowager interjected, 'three,' indicating herself.

Darcy said, 'four' and pointed at Georgiana.

Lady Susan said, 'even better.' She then looked searchingly at Charlotte. 'Miss Lucas...'

'Please call me Charlotte,' interjected the lady.

'Very well, Charlotte, and you may as well call me Aunt Susan since you will be family. But as I was going to ask, have you been presented at court?' When Charlotte agreed, she said, 'excellent. That means we can dress you in strong colours. Those pastels you are wearing make you look washed out. You need something vibrant to bring out your beauty.'

At Charlotte's stunned look, Elizabeth laughed. 'I have been trying to tell you so for years, but you would not listen.'

'Thank you, Aunt Susan, Grandmother. I place myself in your hands.' Charlotte capitulated.

~~DL~~

The names of Denton, Fitzwilliam and Darcy gained them appointments at the dates and times of their choosing, starting the following day.

Before they visited the modistes, Elizabeth suggested a visit to Jane's Uncle Gardiner's warehouse.

'He has the most stunning fabrics and lace. And by buying from him direct, we will save a significant amount. Considering how many dresses we are getting; it is the sensible thing to do.' She added with a sly grin at Charlotte, 'the savings will pay for the bulk of Charlotte's wardrobe.'

Charlotte looked very relieved at the statement. She had confided to Elizabeth that she felt very uncomfortable to accept the Dowager's largesse.

The ladies spent a delightful afternoon in the Gardiner warehouse, choosing fabrics. Charlotte was stunned at the number of fabrics being selected for dresses for only four ladies.

~~DL~~

The following day they started the round of visiting modistes. Day dresses, walking dresses, evening dresses, ball gowns as well as all the relevant accessories.

Elizabeth was grateful that three years previously, her grandmother had gifted her with a new wardrobe for her coming out. At least this time she was not required to hold still for quite as many fittings.

But she could, and did, sympathise with Charlotte who was getting ready to scream when she was presented with yet another set of fashion plates in the latest style.

'Good heavens, I have no wish to look like I have been tarred and feathered,' exclaimed Charlotte in shock.

Madam Beaumode chuckled, 'Miss Lucas, this is the latest fashion. I did not suggest it is in good taste. But many ladies insist on being fashionable at all costs.'

The modiste schooled her features back into a polite smile. 'I am gratified that you have excellent taste. I will not have to compromise my integrity by producing dresses in what *I* consider to be bad taste.'

Charlotte blushed, both for her outburst and the compliment. 'I would like my dresses to be elegant and comfortable; in styles that are fashionable, as long as that style flatters me and is not over-ornamented.'

'In that case, I think you will like these styles.' She brought out another set of plates.

All the ladies agreed these styles were much more suitable not only for Charlotte but for all of them.

Madam Beaumode was a very happy woman. 'With four ladies from the first circles being dressed elegantly and in good taste, we may set a new trend.'

She missed the look the Dowager gave Charlotte which said, '*I told you so.*'

~~DL~~

When they were not busy selecting styles and matching fabrics to their choices, being measured or fitted, the ladies spent most of their time in discussion. The location varied as the ladies took turns hosting their friends.

The first time Charlotte came to Denton House, she was stunned. 'Grandmother, you and the others always referred to Denton House as the townhouse. But this is a mansion, not a townhouse.'

'It is a house, and it is in town. Therefore, it is a townhouse.' The Dowager shrugged. 'You must also keep in mind, this is the town residence of a Duke, who at times is required to host a great many people. That requires space.'

Charlotte was learning a great deal, and not just about what was expected of her as a duchess from two of the grand dames of society.

Charlotte had one burning question. 'Grandmother, how can you always get your way?'

'I suppose it is because I have had almost half a century to grow into my role. I am so used to people obeying me, that I simply assume they will obey me. That automatic assumption carries a lot of weight, which makes most people automatically obey me. It is like a self-fulfilling prophecy.' She grinned. 'In ten years at the most, you will be used to being obeyed as well.'

Charlotte looked doubtful but had no arguments to present since she lacked the experience.

~~DL~~

Once the first day dresses were delivered, her circle of teachers expanded to include Lady Cordelia Worthington, Lady Sefton, and Lady Beatrice, the Countess of Marven.

The Dowager was delighted when Alistair had introduced Lady Beatrice to their circle. They had become instant friends.

Charlotte was surprised when much of what she learned had nothing to do with etiquette or even managing a large household but was background information about the various people she was likely to meet. Her love of reading about history paid dividends since she was already familiar with many of the names and their official history.

Some people would have called it gossip, but in this case, it was essential that Charlotte learned which subjects to avoid with certain people as well as which subjects would be welcome to discuss. The ladies wanted to ensure that she would not make a fool of herself, as she had feared, by saying the wrong thing to the wrong person at the wrong time.

'It is a game,' explained Lady Sefton, 'an exquisite dance. As long as you know the rules or the steps, you cannot go wrong. Do not worry; you have the support of your family and friends.'

'I have come to realise that Lady Amelia is a force of nature,' Charlotte now grinned. 'I do not believe anyone could stand against her.'

'I have never heard her described in those terms, but you are very perceptive,' agreed Lady Susan.

~~DL~~

Amongst all this activity, the Dowager ensured that Alistair would get time to spend with Charlotte.

The first time he saw her in one of her new dresses, he was stunned. 'My dear, I always knew you are beautiful, but this colour makes you look absolutely stunning. I am exceedingly happy you have agreed to be mine; otherwise, I would have to wade through all the single gentlemen in town to get to you.'

Charlotte's blush of pleasure was almost as deep as the deep red of her new dress.

They often had family dinners with the Darcys, which gave Alistair and Charlotte the opportunity to have private conversations. The family gave them the space they needed to speak privately, although they were in the same room.

On days when Charlotte felt particularly overwhelmed, spending an hour in quiet inconsequential conversation with Alistair, was the balm she needed.

Alistair, on the other hand, was thrilled that she looked to him for support and a respite from the pressures of becoming a member of his social circle.

On one of those days, when she felt particularly downhearted, Charlotte said to Alistair, 'I still do not understand what you see in me. There are much more beautiful women out there who would be only too thrilled to be your wife.'

'You mean my duchess. Most women want to marry the title, not the man. They see it as an opportunity to lord it over the other ladies in town,' replied Alistair. 'How do you feel about living in town?'

'I am used to living in a small country town, and I am not certain how I can cope with living in the city.'

'You prefer the country?' asked Alistair.

'I certainly do. In Meryton there are four and twenty families. We all know each other, and we are mostly all friends. Here, on the other hand...'

'I too prefer living in the country, with a small and friendly social circle. I only spend time in town when I need to attend to business or to visit grandmother. She has been living in town because it was more central for all her family. But I believe she too prefers the country. How would you feel if she lived at Denton Manor?'

'I would be delighted to have her company. Having her there to give me advice would be invaluable.'

Alistair could not resist teasing, 'so you prefer my grandmother's company over mine?'

'Never!' exclaimed Charlotte while she blushed. Although the main reason for her blushes was her reaction to Alistair tracing circles with his thumb in the palm of her hand which he was holding.

~~~oo0Ooo~~

After the first flurry of activity of acquiring Charlotte's wardrobe and introducing her to her mentors, the Dowager suggested that the rest of Charlotte's education could be just as easily accomplished at

Netherfield rather than London, where the air in summer was unpleasant, to say the least.

However, before they left for the country, the Dowager decided it was time to tease the *ton*.

'I think an evening at the theatre is in order,' she declared one afternoon while they were having tea with Lady Susan.

'I believe 'A Midsummer Night's Dream' is playing tomorrow night,' suggested Elizabeth, who had been keeping an eye on the program since she loved the theatre.

'An excellent choice, would you all join us in our box?' offered the Dowager.

'You want me to appear in public?' asked Charlotte with some trepidation, although the idea of seeing a performance at the theatre excited her.

'Yes, I want you to be seen with Alistair before we leave for the country. That will set tongues wagging, and speculation will be rife when we return in autumn for the Little Season. At which point, we will announce your engagement.'

'You want me to wait another three months before I can tell the world?' Alistair protested.

'Yes, because that will fit with the story. A friend of Lady Elizabeth Darcy came to town for a visit. Because of the family connection, you two met. When the lady left again for the country, you followed to court her. After a perfectly respectable period of three months, you become engaged. That way, there is no possible suggestion of Charlotte chasing you,' explained the Dowager.

'The first step is to be seen at the theatre.'

~~~oo0Ooo~~~

The following evening the Dowager and Alistair picked up Charlotte and the Darcys. Charlotte looked stunning and regal in a silk dress of a deep red that bordered on purple.

Alistair thought his beloved looked perfect. The Dowager was a little more critical. 'I believe this outfit needs one more touch to be perfect.' She reached into her reticule and extracted a small silk pouch which she handed to Charlotte.

Charlotte opened the pouch and tipped the contents into her hand. She stared in disbelief at the delicate gold chain with an exquisite solitaire diamond pendant. 'You want me to wear this?'

Alistair looked at the jewel and said to his grandmother, 'this is part of your personal jewellery, is it not?'

'It is, and I have not worn it in at least thirty years.'

'I think it is the perfect choice,' he said as he took the chain from Charlotte's unresisting fingers and stepping behind her, clasped the necklace around her neck.

Now the Dowager nodded agreement, 'Perfect. We are now ready to go.'

Alistair entered the theatre with the Dowager and Charlotte on his arms, followed by Elizabeth and Darcy. In the foyer of the theatre, they were greeted warmly by The Earl and Countess of Matlock, who joined the party in their box.

Since it was the end of the season, many people had already left for the country, but there was still enough of an audience to mark the attendance of the Dentons and notice Alistair's attention to Charlotte.

During the intermission, a few curious people tried to get an introduction to Charlotte but were fobbed off with a comment that the lady was a dear friend of Lady Elizabeth Darcy.

~~DL~~

The following week the party bound for Netherfield left London. Charlotte left the bulk of her new wardrobe in London, to avoid awkward questions by her family. 'You can tell your mother that these dresses were a gift from Elizabeth and myself, to ensure you would not feel underdressed while you were in town,' suggested the Dowager.

The Darcys decided to spend a few weeks at least at Pemberley, giving Elizabeth a chance to see her new home and establish herself as Mistress.

The Earl and Countess of Matlock expected to visit with Richard and Jane at Longbourn.

Lady Francine was agreeable to host Charlotte's mentors and had invited Lady Sefton and Countess Marven to spend the summer at

Netherfield. Lady Sefton had declined since she already had other commitments but promised to visit.

Since the Countess of Marven had time on her hands and enjoyed the challenge to help the next Duchess of Denton, she accepted the invitation to spend a month at Netherfield. In the meantime, she stayed in town to direct some very careful rumours.

~~DL~~

23 Surprise

With the end of summer arrived the start of the 'Little Season'. The Dowager and Countess Marven decided that Charlotte was ready to tackle London Society.

The summer had been sheer torture for Alistair. He wanted to shout from the rooftops that he had found his perfect partner. But he understood the necessity to establish Charlotte as a woman of consequence.

Charlotte had spent much of the summer at Netherfield, ostensibly because the Dowager enjoyed her company. In reality, while she spent most of her time with the Dowager and Lady Beatrice, learning about her future role, she also had the opportunity to get to know her intended.

One day she laughed, 'I had always maintained that it is best to know as little as possible about the man I would marry. I now find that I rather like getting to know you.'

'Why did you not want to know your husband before your marriage?' Alistair was curious.

'I did not want to have unrealistic expectations of felicity because, for many years, I did not expect to marry for love. Whereas now, I can hardly wait to be married.' She raised his hand, which she was holding and brushed his knuckles against her cheek. She was rewarded by a small gasp from her beloved.

~~DL~~

At last, the day arrived when the Dowager judged that the time was right to make the engagement public.

Charlotte and Alistair were having tea with her when she broached the subject. 'I had a letter today from Lady Sefton. She tells me that there are some very favourable rumours in town about you courting a friend of Lady Elizabeth Darcy. She is rumoured to be a very genteel and accomplished lady whom you had to persuade to consider you. It is now safe to speak to Sir William Lucas.'

'I will get changed at once. After all, I should be at my best when I ask your father for your hand,' Alistair said to Charlotte and rushed from the room.

The Dowager turned to Charlotte. 'I hope you do not feel ill-used that we kept this from your family?'

'No, grandmother, I always understood. Father could never have kept quiet if he had known I was to be married to the Duke. He will be over the moon at the honour. But I had better take some smelling salts with me, to have on hand when we tell my mother,' Charlotte replied with twinkling eyes.

Alistair managed to get changed in record time. Not long afterwards the couple were in the Denton carriage with the Dowager acting as chaperone.

When they arrived at Lucas Lodge, Lady Lucas was happy to see the Dowager again, who had visited on several occasions over the summer and offered refreshments. The Dowager accepted while Alistair asked to speak to Sir William in private.

'Your Grace, it is good to see you again, but I cannot think of any reason why you need to speak to me in private,' said a very puzzled Sir William, when they had entered the small parlour, he used when he wanted some privacy.

Alistair realised that he had forgotten the speech he had rehearsed for weeks. Instead, he simply said, 'Sir William, I will come straight to the point. Over the last several months I have come to know and love your daughter Charlotte. I would like to ask for your blessing and her hand in marriage.'

Sir William stared at the Duke in open-mouthed disbelief. When he had not responded for a full minute, Alistair became concerned. 'Sir William, are you well? Can I get anything for you?'

Sir William Lucas shook himself out of his stupor. 'By Jove. You wish to marry Charlotte?' he questioned.

'I do, Sir,' replied Alistair.

'I need a drink,' Sir William said as he went to a sideboard and poured a hefty measure of brandy into a glass. After swallowing a generous mouthful, he asked, 'why would you want to marry Charlotte? She is seven and twenty years old, she is nothing much to look at, and she has only a very small dowry.'

'Because she is kind, intelligent and an excellent conversationalist. She likes me for myself and not my title. And you are quite wrong about her looks. I think she is very beautiful.' Alistair did not appreciate Sir William belittling his beloved.

Sir William was startled by the vehemence of the Duke's response. 'Are you sure...' he said hesitantly.

'Quite sure.'

'Of course, you have my blessing, Your Grace.' Sir William conceded. 'You just caught me by surprise. I simply had not expected a man of your consequence to be interested in my daughter.'

He was coming back to being himself. 'Capital. This is just capital. Lady Lucas will be thrilled. We must go at once and give her the good news.' He rushed back to the parlour where the ladies were gathered. Alistair followed more slowly.

'Lady Lucas, you will never believe what just happened,' Sir William exclaimed.

The Dowager smiled at Charlotte, who reached into her reticule to extract the smelling salts.

'What is it, Sir William. What will I not believe?' his wife asked slightly alarmed at his demeanour.

'His Grace just asked for Charlotte's hand,' cried her husband.

'You mean, as in marriage?' she asked in wide-eyed astonishment.

'Yes, as in marriage. He wants to make our Charlotte his duchess.'

'Charlotte a duchess. Oh dear.' Lady Lucas was overcome with emotion and as predicted, swooned.

Her daughter was beside her in an instant with the salts at the ready. It did not take long for the lady to recover.

'Charlotte, is it true? Will you truly be a duchess?' Lady Lucas asked.

'Indeed, she will be, Lady Lucas,' replied Alistair.

'But oh, what will people think if you marry a plain and penniless spinster. They will think she compromised you...' Lady Lucas was quick to consider the potential realities of the situation.

'There is no need to worry, Lady Lucas, the situation is under control,' declared the Dowager. 'It is well known in the right circles that my grandson has been courting your daughter for months.'

'If he has been courting her for months, why did he not come to me earlier?' Sir William was getting upset.

Lady Lucas looked measuringly at the Dowager and at her husband. 'Dear Sir William, could you have been discreet about their courtship?' she asked.

Her husband looked startled but calmed down and after a moment looked chagrined, 'I would have been too excited.' He nodded and addressed the Dowager, 'I guess this needed careful handling to ensure that my daughter's reputation is not tarnished. I would have been like a bull in a china shop.'

'I am grateful that you understand, Sir William,' the Dowager soothed. 'We did not wish to keep you in the dark, but you are too honest for the machinations of the *ton*.'

Sir William now smiled ruefully. 'I suspect you are quite right. But what happens now? I presume you have a plan?'

'Now we will send advertisements to the papers, announcing the engagement of Alistair Flinter, the Duke of Denton to Miss Charlotte Lucas of Meryton. Good friend of Lady Elizabeth Darcy. Next week she will accept an invitation from her good friend in London. My grandson and I will also remove to London,' the Dowager explained.

She started to grin. 'Then we will introduce the happy couple to society and listen to the anguished screams of all the matchmakers when they realise that the Duke of Denton is off the marriage mart.'

Sir William and Lady Lucas burst out laughing albeit in a slightly hysterical fashion.

~~DL~~

24 Introductions

The following week, the Dowager and the newly engaged couple were bound for London again. This time they had an additional travelling companion. Lydia was also to stay at Darcy House to keep Georgiana company while her sister and brother were busy supporting Charlotte's introduction to the wider London society.

When they arrived, they found that Georgiana was bouncing on her toes in excitement to see her friend again. As soon as the party was inside the house and the doors were closed, she threw propriety out the window and rushed to Lydia to engulf her in a fierce hug. 'It is so good to see you again. You have the room next to mine. Come, let me show you. I have so much to tell you. Letters are simply not enough.'

Elizabeth and Darcy looked on with indulgent smiles. It was good to see Georgiana so lively. When Lydia shot her sister a questioning look, Elizabeth nodded her approval. Lydia needed no second invitation, she followed Georgiana upstairs.

Elizabeth greeted her friend and her family almost as effusively. 'We also have much to tell you,' she beamed.

'Very well. If you have a seat that is well padded and does not bounce around, I will be happy to hear what you have to say,' the Dowager replied for all of them.

When they had settled in the drawing-room with refreshments, Elizabeth explained, 'Aunt Susan visited yesterday. It seems that the announcement of your engagement caused quite a stir with some people.'

Elizabeth's eyes twinkled. 'But when you have three preeminent countesses supporting the match, very few people will have issues. You know how Aunt Susan can be. "Of course, I know Miss Lucas. I wondered how long it would take the Duke to make his case," or "It is about time the Duke persuaded Miss Lucas to accept his suit," or "Miss

Lucas, daughter of Sir William is a lovely lady and a dear friend of my niece, Lady Elizabeth Darcy".'

Elizabeth's mimicry caused laughter from the whole group. In the case of Charlotte, very relieved laughter.

'Lady Sefton has been telling everyone that grandmother favours the match and that she has known Charlotte for years, from her association with me. Lady Beatrice, on the other hand, was full of stories how Alistair has avoided compromises for a decade and that he is too experienced to be caught. The only reason he would ever marry is for a true love match with a woman of impeccable character.'

Darcy smirked as he bowed to the Dowager. 'General Denton, your strategy was faultless as always.'

'I had some very capable officers to carry out the offensive,' the Dowager went along with his joke. 'Thank you, Lieutenant.'

The Dowager became serious again. 'Are there any negative rumours out there?'

'Yes, there are a few. But considering they are all from women who had hoped to catch Alistair, people are not taking them seriously. Especially with all the support Charlotte has.'

'Good. In that case, I will go home. I have already sent out invitations to the other ladies to join me for lunch tomorrow. I suggest you do the same.'

~~DL~~

'Ladies, I cannot thank you enough for your efforts on my behalf,' said Charlotte to the assembled Countesses.

They had gathered at Denton House for a leisurely lunch and strategy session.

'Think nothing of it, my dear,' replied Lady Beatrice. 'I have been happy to help. Alistair has always been a dear boy, and I am delighted that he has found a woman who likes him for himself.'

Alistair squirmed at being called a dear boy but managed to suppress his blushes. He was sitting next to Charlotte and without realising it, was holding her hand.

Lady Susan said, 'we thought that over the next few days we would take turns to take you along while we call on various friends and acquaintances. We should also, as a family, visit the theatre and the opera.'

'I have brought unlimited vouchers to Almack's for you.' Lady Sefton took her turn.

'I have already started preparations for an engagement ball. I was just waiting to finalise the date. The invitations can go out tomorrow.' The Dowager brought out a sheet of paper. 'Here is the list of people I thought to invite. Do you have any suggestions for changes?'

'When did you have time to arrange a ball?' Charlotte was startled.

'About two months ago,' grinned the Dowager.

'Of course, you have always believed in forward planning.' Alistair shook his head and smiled in admiration.

The countesses just nodded. They expected nothing less from the Dowager Duchess.

Lady Beatrice suggested, 'you should also invite the Duke of Langford. I know he is somewhat crotchety and considered by some to be a curmudgeon, but his wife was the daughter of a minor country gentleman, and he was happily married for many years. He also has some strong views about what he calls the *inbreeding of the aristocracy*.'

'Is he not the grandfather of George and Patrick Langston?' asked Alistair.

'He is indeed. Do you know them?' replied Lady Sefton.

'They started at Cambridge the last year we were there. I did not have much to do with them, but they seemed to be decent chaps. At the time, they did not run with the fast crowd.'

'They turned out to be quite charming and generally well-behaved young gentlemen,' supplied Lady Beatrice.

'I have not seen the Duke since his wife died years ago. He is a good choice. And in that case, I think I will invite the grandsons as well. The girls will be here and will need some decent dancing partners,' decided the Dowager.

~~DL~~

The next weeks were hectic for Charlotte and Alistair, who accompanied her whenever he could. Sometimes he was told his presence would hinder more than help.

Charlotte felt that the countesses dragged her from pillar to post. She looked forward to Sundays when she did not have to socialise, but after church services could spend the day with her intended and his family. Admittedly it was the extended family, but they were all easy to be with.

Every other day she paid calls on various people with her mentors. The other days, she received visitors, either at Darcy, Matlock, or Denton House.

Then there were the dinners and the theatre and the opera.

Luckily for her peace of mind, the majority of people were pleasant and welcoming, largely due to the work of the countesses over the summer.

But then there were some young ladies, who had hoped to snare the Duke, who were not as amiable.

'You must have worked very hard to catch the interest of the Duke,' sniped Miss Smith.

'As a matter of fact, I was trying to discourage him, but he persisted in his pursuit,' replied Charlotte. 'I had only thought of him as my friend's cousin, not as a potential husband.'

'You cannot expect me to believe that you did not wish to be a duchess. Why ever would you not?'

After days of conversations like these, Charlotte's temper finally snapped. 'Because I knew that as a duchess, I would have to deal with people like you.'

Miss Smith blushed in embarrassment, then mumbled some excuse and took herself off to less perceptive company.

Afterwards, Charlotte felt mortified that she had lost her temper. Alistair reassured her. 'Miss Smith is known for her rudeness and vicious gossip. You are not the first lady to put her in her place. But she never learns.'

'Who else would say anything as outrageous as I just did?' Charlotte asked a rhetorical question.

To her surprise, Alistair answered, 'Jane Bennet.'

'Jane Bennet? Truly?'

'Truly. It was at a ball the year she and Elizabeth were presented. Miss Smith made some disparaging remarks about Elizabeth, and Jane gave the lady a dressing down that rivalled anything grandmother could do. It made her known as the Avenging Angel.' Alistair grinned.

'If even Jane Bennet can lose her temper with that woman, I do not feel quite as bad,' Charlotte admitted.

In the background, the Dowager had also observed the exchange. She was very pleased to see that Charlotte would stand up for herself and, when necessary, would put people in their place. After all, a duchess had many people looking to and depending on her. She needed to be strong enough not to be overwhelmed, either by people or situations.

~~DL~~

One memorable evening was spent socialising at Almack's. Unfortunately for Charlotte, it was mainly memorable for the sheer boredom engendered by the conversation.

Although Charlotte was now very fashionably dressed, she had no particular interest in fashion. But she rose to the occasion. At least it was a more varied topic than the weather. Although one lady did not appreciate Charlotte's innocent honesty.

'You must give me the name of your dressmaker. Your gown is reminiscent of the style favoured by Madam Beaumode, although not quite what *I* usually get from her,' commented the lady in a supercilious tone.

'You are very perceptive to discern that the style of this dress was Madam Beaumode's since it is a design which she reserves for ladies who wish to be elegant, without being a slave to a fashion which does not suit them,' Charlotte replied casually. 'I believe she has excellent taste.'

Charlotte was much happier to discuss the theatre.

'Miss Lucas, did I not see you at the theatre back in June?'

'If it was at a performance of 'A Midsummer Night's Dream', you could have seen me,' she acknowledged. 'It was a wonderful performance. I particularly enjoyed watching Tatiana. She was exquisite at portraying someone quite otherworldly.'

'Did you see any other plays?'

'Unfortunately, I did not have time to indulge myself. I went home to the country but two days later.'

'But why did you not stay in London? It is such a great city.'

'It is a great city, I agree, but the air in the summer is unpleasant, to say the least. I quite understand why everyone who can, does leave for the country during that time.'

It seemed the weather was not always a safe topic, after all.

~~DL~~

Unbeknownst to Charlotte, Alistair also came in for some attention from someone he had no wish to associate with.

Miss Simpson had come as the guest of a naïve friend who appreciated her knowledge of society. Since the former Duke of Denton had chosen not to make her failed compromise public, and she had been lucky at the lack of physical consequences of her actions, she was still welcome amongst her circle of friends.

To her misfortune, even her considerable dowry had still not resulted in an offer of marriage, due to her personality and lack of consequence. At the age of two and twenty, she was getting desperate to catch a husband.

She decided at one more try for the Duke.

After trapping Alistair in the usual social chat, she simpered, 'Your Grace, I do not understand why you would let the machinations of an unknown country Miss trap you into an unwanted marriage,' while artfully placing a hand on his wrist. 'I am certain you could get out of the engagement.'

Alistair looked down at her hand in disgust and immediately pulled his hand away from her.

'Madam, there are several things you should be aware of. One, Miss Lucas is a lady of impeccable character who would not stoop to the machinations which are common amongst the social climbers in town. To suggest otherwise is defamation, which is punishable by law.' Miss Simpson gasped at his words, due to the ramifications to herself and the venom in his voice.

'Two, I feel honoured that Miss Lucas has consented to become my wife. And finally, I have no interest in used goods. I particularly object to my father's castoffs.' He abruptly turned his back on her and walked away, leaving behind a mortified Miss Simpson.

~~DL~~

25 Preparations

A few days later, a convoy arrived from Denton Manor. The lead carriage contained Mrs Anne Hopkins, the Dowager's companion, who had been visiting with family while the Dowager was busy, first with Elizabeth's wedding and then with Charlotte's education. Anne's family owned a small estate neighbouring Denton Manor.

When the Dowager first started to arrange the ball, she had delegated Anne Hopkins to supervise the mustering of materials and personnel which could be supplied by the estate.

Now there was one cart containing carefully packed glass and dinner ware, linen, as well as cookware and utensils. The other carts ferried fresh produce to provide the finest meal that could be had for the ball, as well as the supplies required to feed a multitude of servants for the week they were to stay in town.

Anne Hopkins shared the carriage with the senior staff from Denton Manor. The majority of cooks, scullery maids, footmen and maids from the estate were squeezed into every other carriage available at Denton, plus several hired chaises.

It was a blessing for all concerned that Denton House was a large building with correspondingly large staff quarters, which usually were at least half empty. It was going to be a tight fit, but the staff's loyalty was such that nobody minded. It also gave them a chance to spend a few days in the capital.

Charlotte, who was visiting at Denton House, stood in awe at the sight of the mass of people and supplies arriving. When the Dowager explained who the people were, she asked, 'is there anyone left at the estate? It looks like every soul from miles around has come to town.'

'Mr Carter, the steward, is still there with a skeleton staff of about twenty people.'

Charlotte swallowed convulsively. 'How big is Denton Manor that you need this many people to maintain it?'

The Dowager shrugged. 'It is a big house, but it is still just a house. I hope your presence will make it a home.'

'Why did you send for all these people? Could we not have just hired extra staff locally?' Charlotte wondered.

'Yes, we could have hired extra hands, but for the ball, I only want staff I trust in the house, in case there are issues. Such as, someone drinks too much and becomes difficult, or if someone behaves inappropriately for any reason. It is best to have discreet people taking care of things.'

'I am still learning that there is more to this position than just socialising with the *ton*,' sighed Charlotte.

'Cheer up, to quote something Thomas once said to Alistair, *It's a Duke's life, but someone has to do it*,' the Dowager said with a grin.

Charlotte shot her a disgusted look, although she did not say whether it was for the sentiment or the horrible pun.

~~DL~~

In the wake of this convoy arrived another which was very welcome to Alistair.

Mr and Mrs Bennet arrived, accompanied by Mary and Catherine as well as Robert.

Robert's time in the country had done wonders for his health. Although his shoulder was still not up to the strain of wielding a sword, the pain was gone, and he was otherwise fully recovered. Being with family who cared for him had also restored his spirits.

Alistair greeted his brother effusively. 'I am so glad that you are here. There has been a sad lack of gentlemen for me to speak to lately.'

'Do not tell me that you are already getting tired of the company of your lovely bride,' Robert teased.

'No, of course not. But her time is being monopolised by grandmother and the other ladies. You know how grandmother is. She is in her element with the introduction of Charlotte and the preparation for the ball. I think it has been a long time since she had so much fun.'

Robert could not help it; he burst out laughing.

~~DL~~

When Charlotte returned to Darcy House, she spotted a familiar face in the hallway. 'Mrs Nicholls, what are you doing here?' she asked the Netherfield housekeeper in surprise.

'Mr and Mrs Bennet brought the family into town for your engagement ball. This freed up most of the staff at Netherfield to help at Denton House. Although, since there is not enough room for everyone, Mr Darcy and Lady Elizabeth have kindly offered to put us up.'

Charlotte was stunned yet again. 'How many more people are coming?'

'If you want to cater a ball properly, it takes one servant for every guest,' explained Mrs Nicholls. She smiled sympathetically. 'You should know that Mr and Mrs Fitzwilliam have come from Longbourn, and they and their staff are staying at Matlock House.'

Charlotte slumped down on the stair next to her and put her head in her hands in despair. 'This is just too much.'

'Cheer up Miss Lucas, you will not have to entertain this many people again for a while.' Mrs Nicholls smiled sympathetically. 'At least until your wedding,' she could not resist to add.

Charlotte looked up sharply at the woman. 'This does not make me feel better.'

She determined to speak to Alistair to see if he would help her persuade the Dowager to agree to a small and intimate wedding with only family and a few close friends.

Then she realised that considering the size of his extended family, and the supporters who had helped her establish herself, that could still be in the vicinity of fifty to one hundred guests.

~~DL~~

While she was still sitting on the stairs, the front door was opened by a footman to admit two people Charlotte was happy to see. Sir William and Lady Lucas had arrived to attend their daughter's engagement ball. They had been invited by Elizabeth and Darcy to stay with them to be close to Charlotte.

Darcy was just coming into the foyer to greet his guests when Lady Lucas saw Charlotte sitting forlornly on the stair. She rushed to Charlotte's side, exclaiming, 'Charlotte, whatever is the matter? You look distraught. Has anything happened?' It was on the tip of her tongue to ask if the Duke had called off the engagement but decided that was not a wise question to ask in such a public setting.

Darcy who had briefly greeted Sir William also came to Charlotte; concern written all over his countenance.

Charlotte shook her head and started laughing somewhat hysterically. 'I just found out that grandmother has arranged for extra servants for the ball,' she explained.

'Why would that upset you? We all hire some extra people when we have a large party.' Her mother was nonplussed.

'But we do not bring in almost all the servants from Longbourn, Netherfield *and* Denton Manor. It has just been brought home to me that the sphere I am entering, lives considerably larger than we do.'

Lady Lucas, who knew how many staff were at her neighbouring estates, asked in consternation. 'How many servants are there?'

'Over three hundred in total.'

'Oh dear,' said Lady Lucas and sat down next to Charlotte.

'The Dowager certainly never does anything by half,' commented Sir William with admiration.

'You do not know the half of it,' muttered Darcy to himself.

~~DL~~

26 Denton Ball

The invitations had been sent out and accepted. The public rooms of the house had been prepared to host three hundred of their closest friends. The cooks had performed small miracles to have a wide variety of dishes in sufficient quantity ready to be finished and served.

Everything was in readiness for the Engagement Ball for the Duke of Denton and his lovely fiancé.

The immediate family had assembled at Denton House earlier in the day. The ladies had decided that it was best if they dressed at the house to safeguard their gowns, Charlotte's in particular.

Everyone would be wearing new gowns. Even Lady Lucas had a new dress made for the occasion from a fashion-plate she received from Mrs Bennet, who also helped her choose the fabric and colour.

Since Charlotte was a good friend of all the Bennet daughters, Lydia was allowed to attend the first half of the ball on the proviso that she danced only with family members. Because Lydia would be at the ball, Darcy had given permission for Georgiana to attend as well, with the same conditions. Both girls were thrilled.

The young women had a lot of fun helping each other get all prettied up. They had maids assisting them, but it was more fun to help each other. For the Bennet sisters, it was quite a nostalgic time.

Charlotte, of course, was the centre of their attention. She, who only had one sister, was now surrounded by six young ladies who were all determined that she would outshine them all.

Elizabeth noticed that Charlotte had become rather quiet. 'What is the matter, my friend?'

Charlotte swallowed back the tears which had threatened and said, 'you are all so incredibly kind. I am used to being the plain Jane, and now I have Jane Bennet trying to make me more beautiful than herself.'

'Charlotte, when will you listen. I have told you for years that you are beautiful, and when you are with Alistair, you positively glow. All that we are doing is gilding the lily just the tiniest bit,' Lizzy grinned at her friend. 'We could dress you in sackcloth, and the moment Alistair takes your hand, you shine to the point that everyone will swear that you are dressed fit to be a queen, never mind a lowly duchess.'

Charlotte looked searchingly at her friend. 'You are serious, I think.'

'I certainly am.'

Charlotte straightened her shoulders and raised her chin. 'Very well. I will believe you.'

'It is about time, granddaughter.' The Dowager looked critically at Charlotte. 'Very good. Now you look almost like a duchess.'

She smiled at Charlotte, 'since you appear to be ready, I need you to come with me for a few moments.'

She led Charlotte to her private sitting room where Alistair was waiting for them.

'You look quite amazing. I will be the envy of every single man at the ball and many of the married ones.' Alistair smiled at Charlotte when he took her hand and raised it slowly to his lips.

When he let go of her hand, he picked up a box from a nearby table. 'I wanted to see you before we go downstairs because I have an engagement gift for you.' He handed her the box.

Charlotte opened the box to discover a complete set of sapphire and diamond jewellery made up of a necklace, a bracelet, a ring, drop earrings and even a delicate tiara. 'These are part of the Denton family jewels. They are always given to the bride of the heir, or if his father is dead, the Duke,' Alistair explained.

'That is why grandmother insisted on royal blue for my gown,' exclaimed Charlotte in sudden understanding.

'I did, and I was exceedingly grateful that that is a colour which becomes you very well. Here, let me help you with these,' the Dowager offered.

Once she was decked out in all her finery, Alistair took Charlotte's hand and led her to a mirror on the other side of the room.

'I think we make a very handsome couple. Do you not agree?'

Charlotte stared in amazement at the remarkably handsome woman who looked back at her. Yes, that woman did look like a duchess.

Then she looked at the reflection of Alistair next to herself and realised, 'your coat matches the colour of my gown exactly.'

Alistair sighed dramatically. 'I am afraid, grandmother likes to coordinate every detail.'

'And now I need to coordinate a receiving line,' agreed the Dowager.

~~DL~~

The receiving line did not take much coordination. All it took was for the three of them to walk downstairs to the foyer. The Dowager had decided it would be easier on Charlotte to keep the number to a minimum. Which meant that the Dowager was there as the hostess of the ball, the Duke for obvious reasons and Charlotte for equally obvious reasons.

The rest of the family drifted down from their rooms and kept them company until the other guests started to arrive.

When Sir William saw his daughter for the first time in all her finery, he stopped and stared at her. 'By Jove. You *are* beautiful. Who would have thought it?'

Alistair smirked. 'I knew it all along,' he said while gently squeezing Charlotte's hand.

Lady Lucas just shook her head and said with a loving smile, 'love certainly becomes you.'

Charlotte found that she only needed a few introductions since she had met the majority of guests over the previous weeks. It was still a nerve-wracking experience for her, but she handled it with aplomb.

'Your Grace, I am so pleased that you have accepted our invitation,' said the Dowager.

'Your Grace, I am honoured you invited me to share this joyous occasion with you,' the Duke of Langford replied with a smile.

'I would like you to meet my grandson, Alistair, the Duke of Denton and his fiancé, Miss Charlotte Lucas. Alistair, Charlotte, I am honoured to introduce to you His Grace, the Duke of Langford.'

151

'I am honoured to meet you, Your Grace,' Alistair acknowledged the introduction with a bow.

'I, too, am honoured to make your acquaintance, Your Grace,' said Charlotte with a respectful curtsy.

'No need to be so formal. It is a pleasure to meet you both. Not least of all because there is at least one young man who does not give a fig about society's bias. I asked around, and I think you have chosen wisely.' The Duke of Langford extended his hand to Alistair, who was happy to shake it.

Langford turned back to the Dowager and proceeded to introduce his grandsons, who had stayed politely in the background.

They all chatted for a minute. Before they moved on to make way for the next guests, the old Duke said to Alistair with a grin, 'let me know if any of the vultures give you a hard time.'

When most of the guests had arrived, the Dowager allowed the three of them a few minutes to rest in a small room set aside for that purpose, before leading them into the ballroom.

The three of them stepped onto the small stage, and the Dowager addressed the assembled guests. 'My Lords, Ladies and gentlemen. I thank you for coming here tonight to help us celebrate the engagement of my grandson, Alistair Flinter, the Duke of Denton to the lovely Miss Charlotte Lucas, daughter of Sir William and Lady Lucas, of Meryton. I will be forever grateful to my granddaughter, Lady Elizabeth Darcy, for introducing her dear friend to her cousin, who in my opinion, has long been in need of a wife.'

Polite laughter met the last statement while the Dowager signalled for the music to start.

Alistair bowed to Charlotte and offered her his arm to lead her to the dancefloor. They lined up to lead the first dance.

'It is now official, you are mine,' Alistair smiled at his fiancée.
~~DL~~
The ball was over, and the guests had gone except for the Darcys who were waiting for Charlotte to accompany them back to their house.

While everyone was congratulating the Dowager on the success of the ball and saying farewell, Alistair pulled Charlotte into the library for a moment of privacy.

'You were magnificent tonight. I was so very proud of you and proud that you have chosen me for your husband,' he told her huskily as he pulled her into an embrace and proceeded to kiss Charlotte to within an inch of her life, with her enthusiastic cooperation.

They broke apart when they heard a quiet chuckle. Darcy looked at Alistair and Charlotte. 'I see you took my advice,' he said to Alistair with a smirk. 'You found your own girl to kiss.'

~~DL~~

27 Happy Ending?

A month later, at St George's on Hannover Square, Alistair, the Duke of Denton married Miss Charlotte Lucas. The ceremony was conducted by a distant cousin, Bishop Flinter.

The lady had been granted her wish, and only family and close friends attended the ceremony – officially.

Because the date of the wedding had not been kept secret and the church was rather large, quite a number of uninvited guests were present as well. Many people from Meryton had made the journey to London to see one of their own become a duchess. Anyone who had a carriage took as many people as would fit.

When Sir William led Charlotte to the altar, she saw a sea of familiar and smiling faces. That was until her attention was very firmly captured by the man waiting for her at the altar.

Alistair was attended by his twin, who on this occasion had dressed differently to his brother. After all, this was one time neither brother wished for a confusion of identities.

Once Sir William placed Charlotte's hand into his, Alistair was only aware of his glowing bride. Despite his distraction, he must have given the right answers, even if Robert had to poke him in the ribs a couple of times because eventually, he heard the Bishop say, 'You may now kiss your bride.'

This was an invitation with which he was only too happy to comply.

When they came up for air, the Bishop said with a smirk, 'it gives me great pleasure to introduce to you the Duke and Duchess of Denton.'
~~DL~~
After the wedding breakfast at Denton House, Alistair and Charlotte escaped to the library yet again for a minute of privacy.

This privacy was interrupted by Elizabeth and Darcy, who were looking for the couple to take their leave.

'What is it about libraries?' Darcy asked Elizabeth with a smirk when they saw the newlyweds in a passionate embrace, but since the couple were oblivious to the company, Darcy closed the door again. 'I do not think they will mind if we do not say goodbye.'

~~DL~~

A few minutes later, Robert came across his brother and new sister just as they were coming up for air.

Alistair noticed his brother in the open door but had no wish to socialise just then. So, he passed on Darcy's advice, 'Go and find yourself your own girl to kiss and leave us in peace.'

I already found her. Robert thought of a certain blond and blue-eyed beauty. *I am just waiting for her to grow up.*

~~DL~~

Books by Sydney Salier

Unconventional

An Unconventional Education (Book 1) – A P&P Reimagining

Unconventional Ladies (Book 2) – A Regency novel inspired by P&P

The Denton Connection

Don't flatter yourself – A P&P Variation

Mrs Bennet's Surprising Connections – Prequel to 'Don't flatter yourself'

It's a Duke's Life – Sequel to 'Don't flatter yourself'. A P&P spin-off

Lady Alexandra's Hunt – A Regency Romance

P&P Variations

Don't flatter yourself – Revisited – The alternate version of this P&P Variation

Consequence & Consequences – or Ooops – A Regency Romance inspired by P&P

Mr Bennet leaves his study – A Regency Romance based on P&P

No, Mr Darcy – A Regency Romance inspired by P&P

Remember – you wanted this – A collection of P&P variations

Surprise & Serendipity – A P&P Variation

You asked for it – A P&P Variation with a twist

Original Works

Lady Alexandra's Hunt – A Regency Romance

Made in the USA
Monee, IL
04 March 2024

54442095R00100